D0429671

EAGLE VALLEY LIBRARY DISTRICT
1 06 0003790254

Bridge to America

Bridge to America

BASED ON A TRUE STORY

Linda Glaser

HOUGHTON MIFFLIN COMPANY
BOSTON 2005

www.houghtonmifflinbooks.com

The text of this book is set in New Aster.

Library of Congress Cataloging-in-Publication Data

Glaser, Linda.
Bridge to America / by Linda Glaser.
p. cm.
Summary: Eight-year-old Fivel narrates the story of his family's Atlantic Ocean crossing to reunite with their father in the United States, from its desperate beginning in a shtetl in Poland in 1920 to his stirrings of identity as an American boy.
ISBN 0-618-56301-6 (hardcover)
1. Jews—Poland—Juvenile fiction. 2. Jews—United States—Juvenile fiction. [1. Jews—Poland—Fiction. 2. Jews—United States—Fiction. 3. Ocean travel—Fiction. 4. Emigration and immigration—Fiction.] I. Title.
PZ7.G48047Bri 2005
[Fic]—dc22

2005004319

ISBN-13: 978-0618-56301-2

Manufactured in the United States of America
QUM 10 9 8 7 6 5 4 3 2 1

Dedication

To Phil,
Thank you for entrusting me with your stories,
for believing in me,
and for being such a bright light all along the way.

And to you, my dear reader,
May you grow up to be like Beryl and like Fivel—with a big heart.

The highest form of wisdom is kindness.

—Yiddish Proverb

CHAPTER 1

I'll never forget that cold afternoon. It's fixed in my head as clearly as Beryl's face and the warm sweet smell of his bakery. Such a smell could fill an empty stomach!

I was heading there right after *heder*—itching to tell him the trick we'd played on our teacher and hoping for a bagel to fill myself up a little. But Lila, a neighbor lady, came rushing up to me on the road.

"Fivel, I heard there's a man at your house." She leaned in too close, smelling strongly of garlic. "Do you know who it is?" Lila always wanted the gossip. So even if I *had* known, I might not have told her. But the only man I could think of was Pa. My heart leaped at the thought. Was it possible?

"I'd better go see" was all I said. Then I raced down the road so fast my own breath had to run to catch up with me.

Pa. That one word thundered through my whole body. Maybe I'd finally meet him. Maybe he had come for us *himself.* I ran so hard, the heels of my feet hit me from behind. Maybe, maybe, we'd soon be with him in America.

I burst into my house and stopped short.

A tall well-dressed man in city clothes was talking to Ma. We'd never had such a rich-looking man in our house before. And no one had ever stepped onto our hard dirt floor with such shiny leather shoes. He was speaking Polish, not Yiddish—our Jewish language. And he did not have the full beard of a Jew. So it wasn't Pa after all. Disappointment weighed on my chest, heavy as a pile of stones. It took me some time to even care enough to listen or wonder why he was here.

"Please understand, Mrs. Myzel." I heard him say. "All of us will benefit." He stroked the side of his nose with his pointer finger. "You, most of all, with one less mouth to feed." He gave a stiff smile showing mostly teeth. Ma set her lips firmly and shook her head. The man frowned. "Mrs. Myzel, as you well know, life does not look promising for Jews in Poland. So far, 1920 does not bode well." He drew a folded paper from his coat pocket, snapped it open, and offered it to her—"Here is my name and address"—not knowing that Ma couldn't read. "You must realize that I can give him a much better life than *this*." He shot an ugly look around our one-room house and down at the hard dirt floor. It made me want to kick him.

Ma didn't take the paper. "Thank you for your concern." She spoke in Polish, clipping each word. "But we're managing." Her face was rigid as she held the door open for him.

He thrust the paper into her hand anyway. "If things get worse for you Jews, and mark my words they will, you'll be grateful you have this. Good day." He turned and left.

Ma quickly shut the door and gave a little shudder.

"Who was that?" I asked.

She didn't answer. Her mouth was set in a thin tight line.

But my sister Kvola spoke up. "That man . . ." her eyes flashed. "He wants to take you!"

"No!" I threw my arms around Ma.

My sister Hannah was bent over our table mending. She hunched into herself even more at Kvola's words. Ma was still glaring at the door.

Just then, my brother, Benyomin, rushed in, his face flushed from running. "That man," he pointed outside. "What was he doing *here?* Did you see his fancy horse and carriage in front of Tomas and Ana's house?"

A horse and carriage! I hadn't even noticed. I'd been in such a hurry to see Pa. I'd barely glanced next door. He must be very rich. I squeezed Ma's arm. Rich people always seemed to get what they wanted.

Kvola narrowed her eyes. "He wants to take Fivel away. His wife wants 'a good little boy.'" She gave a stiff smile like his—full of teeth.

"What?" Benyomin looked at Ma. "He can't do that!"

"Don't let him!" I clutched Ma around the waist. *"Please."*

"Of course not," said Ma impatiently. "I'm already one child poorer." A shadow of sadness swept behind her eyes. I didn't know what she meant by that. But it wasn't comforting. She drew her mouth into that tight line again as if she'd said more than she'd meant to. She gave Hannah and Kvola a sharp warning look.

"But Ma, what if he comes back?" I cried.

Ma shook her head. "Don't worry." Yet she sounded more tired than reassuring. She set the paper on the table.

That troubled me. I badly wanted to crumple it into a tight ball, throw it into our clay oven, and watch it burst into flames. But something about the heaviness in Ma's shoulders made me uneasy. Now my shoulders sagged, too.

"Pff!" Kvola made a spitting sound. "Don't even think about him! He's gone." She gave a strong kick in his direction as if she, herself, had booted him out of our house. That made me smile. "Don't you worry, Fivel." She tugged my shoulders back up. "Everything will be fine."

I nodded. "Soon we'll be safe in America." I tried to sound just as strong and sure as she did. I looked up at Ma. "Won't we?" I asked, hoping maybe she'd talk about Pa and America like she used to when I was little. But Ma was in her own thoughts. She wiped her hands on her apron and turned to the pot on the stove.

"Soon Pa will send for us." I tried again, enjoying the

sound of those words in my mouth, as though saying them aloud would bring the time closer.

But Ma wasn't in a talking mood. She ladled out our soup for tonight—mostly water with some potatoes and onions, leaving the rest in the pot for tomorrow.

"It's almost *Shabbos,*" she reminded me, feeding a few more sticks to the fire. "Here." She handed me the pot. "Quick to Beryl's. And come straight home before sundown."

I lifted the latch and hurried into the sharp autumn air and down the dirt road. An icy gust swept through my clothes. I shivered, but not only from the cold. That man in city clothes gave me chills. And what about Ma? One child poorer? It made no sense. But why had she looked so sad?

I walked as fast as I could without spilling our soup. I tried to shake off the man's parting words but they clung like burrs. *You'll be grateful you have this.*

"No!" I shouted into the cold wind. "No we won't!"

CHAPTER 2

Other children were rushing to Beryl's with their soup pots, too. Some had a potato or carrot to leave in exchange for a loaf of Sabbath bread. I wished I did even though I knew it didn't matter to Beryl. He gave all of us Sabbath bread whether or not we had anything to give him in return. Like Ma always said, "Beryl the baker is a real *mensch.*" A real fine person. Even so, I wished I had *something* to give him.

I pushed open the bakery door and gulped in the smell of fresh bread. What a smell. Even if that man were the richest in Poland, *he* would be jealous of *my* nose right now. So there.

"Fivel!" Beryl's whole face filled with light. That's what I'd been looking forward to after *heder* today, that look and the story I'd been itching to tell him. The afternoon seemed so long ago by now with such big thoughts weighing on me. But I must try to believe Kvola, that everything would be all right. I set our soup pot on the counter and climbed onto the tall wooden stool next to Beryl's big brick oven—my favorite place in the world, especially now with winter coming.

"Fivel, how was *heder*? You didn't come by today. *Nu?*" So?

I surely wouldn't mention Lila or that man. I'd stay safely away from all that. I settled into my seat welcoming the chance to think about something else—something that would hopefully make Beryl laugh.

"You know how mean our *heder* teacher is," I eased into my story. "He whacks us with a big stick when we lose our place." Beryl nodded. "But," I went on, getting into the mood. "Did you know that sometimes he falls asleep?" I swung my legs, delighting in Beryl's look of surprise.

"What an exciting class!" A smile twitched around the edges of his mouth.

"Today it was, *especially* when he fell asleep. His head went down like this." I drooped my head for a moment. "Then, very quietly, I tiptoed over and lifted his beard like this." I showed, pretending to carefully lift the beard of my snoring teacher. "And *then* . . ." I gave Beryl a gleeful look. "Lahzer and Shmuel glued it to the desk with some thick black wagon-wheel grease."

Beryl chuckled. "You *maziks*." You little mischief makers.

I grinned. "Don't tell Ma. But you should have seen! We waited until it was all set. Then I gave the table a loud *klop*. And he woke up like this—" I jerked my head up and bulged out my eyes, "Owwee!" I grabbed my chin as if in pain.

Just as I'd hoped, Beryl burst out laughing. "Your poor teacher!" He laughed so hard he had to wipe the tears away. Oh, it felt good to make him laugh like that. There was no place in the world I would have rather been right then—maybe not even with Pa in America. "You little *maziks*!" he said again and shook a finger at me. "Wait 'til your ma hears about this." But his smile gave him away. He handed me two Sabbath candles and a loaf of bread. "Now do me a favor and take these to her." I slid the candles into my pocket and held the bread against my chest, letting its warmth soak in.

Already, my mouth was watering. *"A dank."* Thank you.

"Ach! Don't thank me." He brushed my words away. "What's mine is yours. I only wish I had more to give." He placed my pot into his big oven with all the other soup pots.

Everyone knew if it weren't for Beryl, we'd all have cold soup tomorrow. He was the only Jew in our *shtetl* rich enough to keep a fire going all night long. And of course, none of us would light a fire on Saturday, the Jewish day of rest. So thank goodness for Beryl and his big oven.

The bread warmed me all the way home. As soon as I opened the door, I noticed that the paper on the table was gone. What had Ma done with it? Tossed it into the fire? Or tucked it away somewhere? Part of me badly wanted to know, but an even bigger part of me didn't. I handed her the candles and the Sabbath bread.

"What would we do without Beryl?" Ma often said this, and it always made me feel lucky and safe. But tonight, maybe because of that rich man, it sent claws into my stomach. What *would* we do without Beryl? No more Sabbath bread or warm Sabbath soup. Is that what Ma meant?

And now it came back to me what that man had been saying to Ma. *All of us will benefit. You, most of all, with one less mouth to feed.* I must try to eat less. But just thinking about it made me even hungrier.

CHAPTER 3

Ma lit the candles and sang the *Shabbos* blessings. Other nights, she simply lit a thin spindle of wood and held it up so we could see while we ate. But tonight, on *Shabbos,* with soup, bread, and candles glowing, our house felt rich. I ate slowly, making it last.

Even after the last drop, we sat at the table soaking in the candlelight. "Ma," I said quietly, trying again to get her talking about better things. "Are there Cossacks in America?" This was one of my favorite questions.

"No." She shook her head with certainty. "Not even one." She swept her hand across the table as if clearing them away like crumbs. "No Cossacks in America." She brushed her hands together—finishing them off. That was the part I liked best. It always cleared away any left-over scary thoughts. But not tonight.

Tonight, a picture of Cossacks flashed in my head—those tall soldiers on big horses with gleaming swords and bullet belts strapped across their chests in thick Xs. Ma always said, *If there's talk of Cossacks, come straight home—they kill little Jewish boys just for sport.* And we always did go straight home. But how safe was our house with only a wooden latch on the door? *Mark my words, things will get worse for you Jews.*

"With no Cossacks, we'll be safe in America," I urged her on.

"Yes," she said but without much spirit. "That's what we've heard."

Safe. It was hard to imagine.

"Now get to bed," she said shortly. And I knew better than to try for more.

I stood on the chair and climbed onto the wide shelf above our clay oven. Benyomin scrambled up after me. Ma handed us a blanket. We snuggled under it. Lucky for us, Hannah and Kvola were too big to fit here anymore. Now they slept in bed with Ma. And Benyomin and I had this—the warmest place in the house—all to ourselves. Tonight, Benyomin didn't even try to shove me against the cold wall. He let me have the best spot—right above the oven. Maybe that man had made him nervous, too.

I gazed into the flames of the Sabbath candles. Like always, I waited until a certain kind of quiet settled over me. Then I closed my eyes and let Pa float into my head. I could never see his face clearly. But I knew it was Pa. And I knew it was America—even though I couldn't see much of it. As always I thought to myself, Maybe right now, Pa is thinking of me. Then I wrapped my arms around him. "*Git Shabbos,* Pa." Good Sabbath.

I guess it was my own Sabbath prayer—not like the ones my *heder* teacher taught us. He only knew the Hebrew prayers in the book. This one was just mine. And I kept it to myself.

But tonight, my very last thought before drifting off to sleep was not about Pa or America. And it wasn't a prayer either. It was that awful question again. What *would* we do without Beryl? It gnawed a hole in my quiet feeling.

Here in Poland, things were getting worse for Jews—just like that rich man had said. There were more *pogroms*—Cossacks ransacking *shtetls,* burning houses, killing Jews. Maybe Beryl would decide to go to America like Pa. We'd heard that in America, anyone could make a better life—even a Jew. No fear of Cossacks or *pogroms*. And plenty of food. It was hard to believe there was such a place. But it must be real because many Jewish men in our *shtetl* had already gone. They'd all promised to send for their families as soon as they earned enough money. And once in a while, money did come for some lucky family. But many of us were still waiting with barely enough food to keep us alive.

How many times had I pictured us finally walking to America? I imagined us crossing a big long bridge—even longer than the big green metal one beyond our *shtetl*—one stretching all the way to America. I figured that's why Pa needed to send us money—so we could pay to cross it.

Then one day I asked Kvola, "How long does it take to walk to America?"

"You must be joking!" she'd exclaimed. "You can't walk to America. There's a big ocean."

"Yes. But can't we walk across the bridge?"

"There is no bridge," she explained. "The ocean is too big for that. You need to take a boat."

I couldn't imagine so much water that there wasn't a bridge to go over it. Even after she told me, whenever I thought of going to America, I always saw a long metal bridge. Somehow, I couldn't get it out of my head. But even Ma said there was no bridge. She said Pa didn't walk to America. He took a boat.

Ma had told me many times about how Pa left soon after I was born, once he saw that I was strong and healthy. That was probably nine years ago by now—maybe more. But still no money. What if Beryl left us, too? He was rich enough to pay for boat passage. And he had no wife or children so he wouldn't have to send any money back. He'd do well in America. But with him gone, we'd starve. Or, even worse, Ma would give me away. Tears pricked the corners of my eyes.

Of course I knew what Ma would say to that. "Bite your tongue. Beryl is right here with us in Vilkomerski. You'll see him tomorrow just as always." And that was true. I would. And tomorrow, as always, we'd have our best meal of the week. I could hardly wait! So now, from thoughts of starving, already my mouth was watering.

CHAPTER 4

The next morning, I hurried back to Beryl's. My empty stomach shouted at me the whole way, "Faster! Faster!"

I pushed the door open and rushed in.

"*Git Shabbos,* my Fivel!" Beryl handed me a bagel. Just what I'd been hoping for!

I took a good healthy bite. It cut the edge off my hunger. I chewed slowly and let the warmth of the bakery wash over me. This was about as close to heaven as I could get and still be here to tell about it. Even the air had a certain peaceful *Shabbos* feeling.

I hopped onto the high stool to enjoy the rest of my bagel. One by one, children rushed in for their soup pots. As they left, they lifted their lids and smiled.

Each pot had something extra—a piece of chicken, chunks of potatoes, or carrots. We never saw Beryl do it. But we knew that the emptiest pots, like ours, always got the most. That way, once a week, everyone had a full stomach.

"Thank you, Beryl. *Git Shabbos,*" children called as they hurried out.

Slowly, I ate my last bite of bagel. Now Beryl handed

me our soup pot. I lifted the lid. There inside were thick pieces of chicken and big slices of carrots and potatoes.

"Good enough to eat, eh?" Beryl winked at me.

"Mmmm." I licked my lips and slid down from the stool.

"So, you'd better get home." He handed me two more bagels.

I stuffed them into my pocket and eyed the counter. Some children had left a potato or two in exchange for bagels.

"Ma wishes she could give you some potatoes," I told him. "And I do, too."

Actually, our sad little potatoes weren't much to talk about. Weeks ago, after the farmers had harvested their crops, Benyomin and I had gone into the potato fields with Ma and dug up whatever we could find—mostly little ones that no one had bothered with. By the time we'd filled our sack, our hands were icy cold and caked with dirt. But, as sorry as those potatoes were, they had to last us through winter.

"Give me potatoes? *Ach!*" Beryl made a face as if tasting poison. "For what?" He shrugged. "For nothing."

"When Pa sends us money, we'll repay you," I told him.

Beryl shook his head. "I don't want your money. You'll need it to get to America." I usually liked to talk about going to America. But today, all I could think of was my question. I tried it in my head, *Are you going to leave us for America, Beryl?* But somehow, it wouldn't come out.

"So get home with that soup already." Beryl opened the door for me.

I walked home slowly, careful not to spill any. As I went, I thought about my question. Would Beryl leave us? Part of me wanted to know, but most of me didn't—just how I felt about that paper from the rich man. I remembered how Ma had shuddered when he'd finally left. Was she afraid that maybe he was right—maybe someday she'd need that paper? Or, even worse, maybe *he* was the reason Ma was one child poorer. That gave me awful chills. I just hoped Kvola was right—that he was gone for good and not to worry.

I pushed open our door and handed the pot to Ma. She closed her eyes like praying. "Thank goodness for Beryl." She opened her eyes and smoothed my cheek. "You should grow up to be like him, my Fivel, with a big heart." I always liked it when she said that. At least *she* thought it was possible even though we all knew I was no angel. But today, I suddenly wondered why Ma was talking to me about growing up. Wouldn't I still be here with her?

She ladled the soup—our one meal today—giving each of us a thick piece of chicken. We ate slowly so it would fill us for the day. I held myself back from asking, as I often did, for the last bit in the pot. Ma mustn't think of me as another mouth to feed.

After the meal, I whispered to Benyomin, "Let's

go play with Yusig." I gave a sly smile. Of course we shouldn't have—especially on *Shabbos.* But Ma wouldn't know what we were up to out there. And like I said, I was no angel. Besides, it was the easiest way I could think of to set my mind in a different direction. So we hurried out.

Yusig was older than us, but he didn't seem like it. He wasn't very smart. Ma said he was born that way and what a pity it was for Ana and Tomas, his ma and pa. The Polish boys all made fun of him even though he was Polish Catholic like them, *and* his family was rich besides. Benyomin and I were the only ones who'd play with him. Maybe that's why Ana was so good to us—always giving us old mittens and socks that Yusig had outgrown. Of course, she didn't know the tricks we played on him or she might not have been so kind.

Once outside, Benyomin grinned. "Let's get ready for Yusig."

We ran around collecting small flat pieces of wood, giggling the whole time. Then carefully, using two long sticks, I carried over a big fat smelly horse dropping from the side of the road. I made sure to get a fresh one. We covered it with the wood so it was completely hidden.

We always hid the same thing. But Yusig never seemed to remember.

Now we went next door and knocked. Mira, his older sister, answered. I'd been hoping she would so I could look at her beautiful face.

"Can Yusig play?" I asked, grabbing the chance to enjoy her soft, creamy skin and her thick, shiny brown hair.

"I'll go get him," she said and was gone.

"You were staring at her again." Benyomin poked me. "You always do."

"I do not!" I gave him a hard shove. But he just laughed.

Soon, Yusig was at the door with his big silly grin.

"Yusig, we have something for you," I told him. And he grinned even bigger. Already, we could hardly keep from snorting with giggles. We led him outside and around the back of our house. "See?" I pointed. "There's a bird in there. Now you try to catch it. Just lift off this piece of wood, see? And then, quick as you can, slap your hand down. If you're really fast, you'll catch that bird."

It was as if he'd never heard me say this before. Still grinning, he lifted the wood. Slap! Right into it. He looked at his dirty hand, puzzled. "No bird?" He made a pinched face at the smell. We fell on the ground laughing. He laughed, too. And that made us laugh even harder. It was so easy to fool him. We couldn't help ourselves. He wiped his dirty hands on his pants and looked up at me. His mouth went sort of quivery like it didn't know which way to go.

"It was just a joke," I told him. "It's funny."

He nodded with a wobbly smile. "A joke." He wiped his hands on his pants some more, then turned toward home.

"At least we play with him," Benyomin said once he was gone.

"Yeah," I agreed. "And we don't *always* trick him either." Anyway, it didn't really matter. He couldn't even remember from one time to the next.

But that night, as Benyomin and I lay on the wide shelf above the oven, ready for sleep, Ma said quietly to Kvola, "We have a problem."

Immediately, I knew it was about Yusig. Somehow, Ana or Mira had found out. Oh, I hated the thought of Mira knowing! Hardly breathing, I leaned closer to listen.

CHAPTER 5

"What is it? What's the matter?" asked Kvola.

"We're almost out of flour," said Ma.

Kvola gasped softly. "Oh, no!"

So, it wasn't about Yusig after all. It was worse. No flour meant no bread.

We didn't ever talk about it, but we knew where our flour came from. Early this fall, for a few extra coins, Ma had carried sacks of wheat to the mill for some of the farmers. Then when the wheat was ground into flour, she'd carried it back. I hated to see her hauling those heavy sacks on her back! It looked like she'd be crushed under them. But meanwhile, with each sack, she let some of the flour spill into the bodice of her dress.

Ma's bread was dark and heavy—mostly potatoes and turnips with a little flour. Stolen flour. Of course she knew that stealing was wrong. But which was worse? To steal or let her children go hungry? Ma had no trouble deciding.

Now, with the flour running out, all we'd have left besides potatoes and turnips was Ma's sauerkraut. Uh, I did not want to think about it. Her kraut was *strong.* Just last week, I'd found a dead mouse in there. Ma had fished it out and tossed it into the road. Of course we kept the kraut. It had to last us all winter. I hoped that's not all we'd eat. My nose wrinkled at the thought.

We *needed* bread. But even if we only had kraut, I wouldn't complain. No matter what, I wouldn't bother Ma about food, I promised myself. Better to go hungry than be given away.

Ma's voice was tired now. As hard as she tried—hauling flour, doing maid's work, serving beer in the *pivne,* whatever work she could find, there was never enough food.

I listened as she spoke quietly. "You know, Kvola, you're not a little girl anymore. You're old enough to go out and work." I leaned closer, not making a sound. Benyomin snored softly. And Hannah was breathing evenly—also asleep. I was glad for her sake she wasn't hearing this. Even though Hannah was the oldest child, Ma would never ask her to go out and work. Hannah was too timid for that.

"We each help as we can," Ma was now saying. "Hannah does her part." And that was true. Hannah had a way with a needle and thread. She did all our mending and sewing. Her work always looked perfect. "And you, Kvola," Ma went on. "You helped us a lot last summer."

"You mean my dancing?" Kvola's voice swelled with

pride. Last summer, she'd gone out all on her own and put on little shows—dancing and singing like a Gypsy. People must have liked it. She often came home with a handful of coins, her face glowing.

"But it's too cold for that now." Kvola gave a shiver. "It's almost winter."

"Naturally," Ma agreed. "I found you different work. There's a Polish woman not far from here who needs help cooking and cleaning—maybe all week if it works out. They're getting ready for their daughter's wedding. I told her I'd send you tomorrow." I could tell from Ma's voice she wished Kvola didn't have to go.

Kvola heard it, too. "I want to help, Ma. Don't worry. Soon we'll have flour."

Hearing that, I drifted off to sleep dreaming of fresh baked bread. But not Ma's dark heavy bread. *Feh!* Tonight, I dreamed of white bread. Rich people's bread.

Ma used to bring home a piece of white bread now and then—a gift from a nice woman she used to work for. That's when I was little. But I still remember. It was like cake. We ate every last crumb. Maybe tomorrow Kvola would bring some home for us.

CHAPTER 6

"Do they have white bread?" I asked Kvola as soon as she came back the next day. I'd been thinking about it all day. My stomach felt like a mouse was gnawing inside.

"Of course they have white bread," said Kvola as she warmed herself by the oven.

Benyomin and I crowded around to listen. But Hannah stayed at the table cutting potatoes for dinner. "They have loaves and loaves of it." Kvola looked to make sure we believed her. We nodded for her to go on. "And, oh, you should see their house. All the rooms have wooden floors—not dirt floors." She made a face at our floor. "And they eat with real silverware, not wooden spoons." Another face.

"So will you bring us a taste of white bread?" I licked my lips, glad that Ma wasn't home to hear me asking.

"I wish!" said Kvola. "But Mrs. Koslowski isn't nice like that lady Ma used to work for." She shook her head. "Not a bit."

"You could sneak a piece," I suggested—glancing at the door to make sure Ma wasn't about to walk in.

"You must be joking!" Kvola exclaimed. "I wouldn't dare. What if she caught me? I'd be out on my ear."

"But they have so much," Benyomin joined in. "She wouldn't miss it. You could just snitch a little for us."

"No." Hannah spoke up, which was unusual for her. She shook her head, the knife resting motionless on the potato for a moment. "It's not worth it."

"Please, Kvola?" I urged. "She'd never know."

"Well . . ." Kvola smiled. "We'll see. Maybe tomorrow—if no one's looking."

"Don't!" Hannah spoke sharply. "She might catch you." She clamped her elbows tightly against herself like a frightened little bird. "I wouldn't chance it."

"Well *I* would," said Benyomin.

"Me too," I agreed. My stomach grumbled. I'd eaten only one piece of Ma's bread all day. Worse yet, it was hard and stale. "I can't chew any more," I'd complained to her this morning before she left. As soon as I did, I remembered my promise to myself and wished I hadn't.

"*Nu?* You've had enough." She gave me a look. "Go out and play. Both of you."

So Benyomin and I had played outside with an old wheel we found. We ran along, hitting it with a stick to keep it rolling. Benyomin did better than me. On my turn, the wheel kept falling. My mind just wouldn't pay attention. It kept sliding back, again and again, to the bread I was hoping for.

Now I asked Kvola, "Do you think they eat white bread in America?"

"It wouldn't surprise me at all." Suddenly she seemed to know everything there was to know about white bread.

Benyomin's eyes grew wide. "Do you think *Pa* eats it?"

I shook my head. "Not Pa. He's saving his money to send for us. He wouldn't spend it on white bread."

Hannah and Kvola gave each other a certain sad look that they always did when I talked about what Pa would do. But they didn't say anything.

"Someday *I'm* going to eat white bread—plenty of it," said Benyomin.

"Me too," I said. *Maybe tomorrow,* I thought to myself.

But the next day Kvola came home empty-handed again. She rushed to explain before we even asked. "I tried to sneak a little piece. But I heard Mrs. Koslowski coming. She's so strict! Like this." Kvola made a pinched face and strutted around with her nose high in the air until we all laughed. "If she found out, *ai, yai, yai,* she'd be angry!"

"But how would she ever find out? She won't miss one little piece," Benyomin urged.

"Just one," I agreed—fearing that Kvola had already decided against it. "Please?"

The next day, when Kvola came home, her whole face was so bruised and swollen I hardly recognized her.

Hannah rushed over to her. "Kvola! What happened?"

Tears rolled down Kvola's face. "I tried to sneak a piece of white bread," she sobbed. Her lip was so blown up it hurt me to look at it. "I hid it here." She patted the bodice of her dress. "But Mrs. Koslowski saw and snatched it." Her swollen lip quivered. "She called me a rotten thief and she beat me." Kvola sucked in a breath. "Then she kicked me out and screamed at me to never come back." Now, Kvola's voice shrank to a tiny whisper. "She called me 'dirty Jew.'"

"Oh, Kvola." Hannah cradled Kvola in her arms. Kvola buried her face into Hannah's shoulder and sobbed. Her whole body shook. Now Hannah was crying, too.

I looked at Benyomin. "We did wrong," I said—loud enough for Hannah and Kvola to hear.

Benyomin nodded. "Very wrong."

Kvola looked up at us, her eyes red and puffy. "You didn't do anything." She sniffed and wiped the tears from her swollen cheeks. "You didn't know."

I could barely look at her bruised face. I took her hand. "But we made you do it, Kvola." Then I thought of Ma. She'd be furious with me—thinking only of my stomach again—not a bit like Beryl with a big heart. The rich man's words came back at me with a sting. *One less mouth to feed.*

Kvola let out a long shaky breath. "Don't worry about it." She sniffed again and shut her swollen eyes. That's when Ma came through the door. Benyomin and I hurried to tell her what had happened before she saw for herself.

She rushed over to Kvola. "Oh, my poor girl." She tenderly washed the bruises with a wet rag. She was so upset for Kvola, she didn't even think to scold us.

"But that's not the worst of it," Kvola burst out. "She didn't pay me! She said I ate my pay! And that's not true. I didn't eat any bread!" She straightened herself up and looked ready to fight. It did my heart good to see some spark back in her.

Ma sighed and shook her head. "It's done with. We'll find a better place for you to work, with decent people." She looked even more tired than usual.

"But what about the money?" Kvola cried. "I worked so hard!"

"There's nothing we can do." Ma patted Kvola's head as if she was still a little child. "Who would believe a poor Jewish girl?" She shrugged. "It's over and done with. Somehow we'll manage."

CHAPTER 7

The days grew colder. Winter sliced through all the cracks in our house. Benyomin and I kept the fire going when we weren't at *heder,* careful not to use too much wood. When the pile got low, we'd go out searching for fallen branches. Ma cleaned houses. Every now and then, Kvola did, too. Slowly her face came back to normal. But for weeks, her purple bruises made me feel guilty. Whenever I found myself longing for white bread, all I had to do was think of those bruises and I'd stop.

Snow came and the world turned bitter cold. Now, when Ma went out to work, she wrapped her feet in rags. When she got home she'd carefully unwrap them—wincing in pain. If only Pa would send money!

Whenever the mail wagon came, I'd check at the mail shack that same day. That way, if there was anything for us, *I'd* be the one to get it. I knew it wouldn't just be a thin envelope with a letter. Ma couldn't read or write. So why send a letter? No. It would be a real package. That was how money came, hidden away in packages—in pants pockets, in the sleeve of a sweater, someplace where no one else would find it. I often imagined coming home with a package like that. Everyone would crowd around to see. And Ma would be so thankful that she hadn't given me away. But ever since the first deep snow, the mail wagon didn't come as regularly.

With things as they were, I didn't complain at all about going to *heder*, not because I was such a scholar, but because the teacher kept the wood stove nice and hot. And even better, he put potatoes in there every morning. By lunchtime, there was a small baked potato for each of us. Even though our teacher was as mean as ever, at least he knew that hungry boys couldn't learn.

Benyomin and I always tried to sit close to the stove. That way we'd stay warm *and* we could grab the biggest potatoes at lunchtime. But with thoughts of potatoes baking, it was hard to keep our minds on anything else. Often our teacher used that big stick of his to whack the lessons into us. We figured it was a small price to pay for potatoes.

At lunchtime, he'd set out a little jar of herring juice to dip them in. We were so hungry that the strong fishy taste didn't even seem so bad. The potato was the best thing about *heder*—that and the wood stove. We went as often as we could.

But today it was too cold and windy out. *Heder* was too far a walk on such a raw day. None of the other boys were going. And of course Benyomin and I wouldn't dare go by ourselves. All of us Jewish boys walked together since a whole gang of Polish boys was always waiting for us along the way. They'd shout, "Rotten Jews with disease on your heads!" Even though none of them could read or write, they could throw insults *and* stones very well. If just the two of us went, they'd beat us up for sure.

It was a good thing for me that yesterday at *heder,* instead of potatoes, we'd each gotten a bowl of pea soup. And actually, I got *two* meals out of it. I'd fished out the peas that weren't cooked all the way through and saved them in my pocket—wet and all—for later.

But Benyomin had finished all of his right then. So now, as I ate my peas from yesterday, he didn't have any. Naturally, he wanted to go to *heder.*

"Let's try to round up some boys," Benyomin kept urging me. "It's not *so* cold out."

"No," I argued back. "It *is* so cold out." I'd already given him some of my peas. But he was still hungry. "You could've saved some like me," I told him. I intended to spend the day eating my peas and staying as close to our stove as I could without getting burned.

"Don't be so lazy," Benyomin said just to bother me. He knew how I hated to be called lazy. Sometimes I secretly wondered if, being the youngest, I got away with doing less than my share. Then I'd try extra hard. But rounding up a bunch of boys to go to *heder* on a bitter cold day like this wasn't anything I needed to do.

"Go round them up yourself," I said to bother him back. "Who's stopping you?" Yet we both knew he wouldn't go alone. He'd never admit it, but he needed me.

Benyomin gave me a poke in the ribs. "Come on!"

Just then, Kvola rushed in. Her cheeks and nose were bright red. "Fivel! The mail's here. I saw the horse and wagon just now."

That was enough to make me jump. No matter how cold it was out there, this was the one job I'd do with all my heart. I put on my wood shoes.

"It's too cold out!" Benyomin whined—not sounding anything like me. He threw a thin kindling stick at me. "Besides, there won't be anything for us. You should know that by now." He'd never said that before. He was just annoyed about *heder.* He threw another stick at me. "Don't you feel stupid going there and asking again and again, *Do we have any mail? Do we have any mail?*"

"Leave him alone," said Kvola. "Lucky for us he still wants to go."

"That's right." Hannah nodded, looking up from her mending.

Kvola put her arm around my shoulder. "What would we do without you, Fivel? All our packages could be stacked to the ceiling in the mail shack by now, and we'd never even know!"

Her teasing didn't bother me. In fact, I liked it. It made me hopeful. "I have such a good feeling about it today," I told them.

"And what else is new?" Benyomin threw another kindling stick at me. "Every time the mail wagon comes, you have 'such a good feeling.'"

"Never mind." Kvola gave Benyomin a hold-your-tongue look. "I wish we all still did."

Hannah nodded. "I hope you won't be disappointed, Fivel."

I dashed out before she could worry away my good feeling. I was so excited, I hardly noticed the cold. Snow stuck to the bottoms of my shoes as I ran, but I didn't waste time kicking it off. Of course, they weren't real shoemaker shoes. Just two flat pieces of wood with heavy fabric scraps glued on top, with space to slide my feet in. Ma had made them for me last winter. By now they were old and worn. But I had on a pair of Yusig's old socks. So I couldn't complain. It was better than Ma's rags.

By now the snow was caked so thick on the bottoms of my shoes that suddenly, I fell over into a drift. I kicked the snow off and picked myself back up—not about to let old shoes bother me when there might be a package waiting. Anyway, I had a plan to get a pair of real leather shoes—maybe as nice as that rich man's. It was a secret I hadn't told anyone.

As I raced to the mail shack, I let myself remember with relish how my plan had started. It was back when I'd last visited the shoemaker. "Come in, little Fivel," he'd greeted me in Yiddish. "I don't charge for looking." He knew that's all I ever did—look around and warm up. But that day, he'd noticed my wood shoes. "Are those all you have for winter?" He'd raised one thick eyebrow. "Just some old scraps?"

That's when I got my idea. "Yes," I told him. "But if I had some *leather* scraps . . ." I hinted to him, looking around. "My sister Hannah knows how to sew very well. She could make some real shoes for me."

"It's not so easy to make shoes," he said gruffly.

"I know," I'd quickly agreed. "But my sister can sew anything."

At that, the shoemaker sort of smiled—just a little around the edges of his mouth. But, for him, that was a lot. "Well, I'll see what I can find. I'm not promising anything. Next time you come, maybe I'll have some scraps for you." He raised that eyebrow again. *"Maybe."*

So ever since then, I'd been planning it all out in my head. Now, running to the mail shack, I let my plan come up full force. Once I got the scraps, I'd bring them home to Hannah and explain how the shoemaker made shoes. I'd been watching him for so long. By now, I knew all the steps. I'd explain to her how to cut them out and sew them. I was sure she could do it. Hannah could do anything with a needle. Oh, they'd look so fine. And they'd keep my feet warm and dry. Benyomin would be awfully jealous.

For a minute I let myself enjoy that thought. And then with a swell of kindness, I figured maybe there'd be enough scraps so he could have a pair, too. But I'd get mine first. Benyomin would have to wait. I knew all about waiting, being the youngest. Oh, if they knew at home that I was thinking like this, how they'd tease me!

Still I couldn't help it. I always got especially hopeful going to the mail shack.

I ran right past the peddler's wagon. It was so cold that long icicles hung from the horse's nostrils. But I was too excited to be cold. Usually, when the peddler came, I liked to stop and see what he had. Not today, though. I ran straight to the mail shack and burst in.

"Is there something for the Myzels?" Already, I could feel how it would be to hold a package from Pa. I'd march straight home with it and hand it to Ma. We'd all watch her open it. There'd be a pile of money inside. All the tired lines on Ma's face would smooth away. Everyone would crowd around, so glad I'd gotten our package before the money was stolen.

It was always bad when a package came for someone torn open. No money. Sometimes I even wondered if maybe Pa had already sent us money, but it was stolen before we ever got it. I hoped he knew to hide the money.

I waited anxiously for the man behind the counter to hand me our package. He glanced down at me. "Nothing for you," he said without even really looking.

"Please check," I begged. If only he'd let me get behind that counter. I'd find it, for sure.

He looked—but not very hard. Not the way I would have.

"Still nothing." He shrugged.

How many times had he said that by now? *Still nothing.* I tried hard not to show how much it hurt. I turned and ran out the door and down the road as fast as I could, far away from that *still nothing.*

But a horrible question snatched at me on the way. Not the usual one, *Does Pa know to hide the money?* This was a new question that sent icicles down my arms and legs. *What if Pa never sends us money?* I'd never considered this before. I wished I could stop myself now. But instead more questions came rushing at me. *Why doesn't Pa send any? Why haven't we heard from him by now? What if he's forgotten us and married someone else?*

A coldness gripped me that was even colder than the icy chill of winter. We'd heard of such things. Lila who loved to gossip always smacked her lips when telling about them. A man leaves and finds a new wife in America. Starts a new life. A whole new family. He forgets all about his family in the *shtetl.*

But no. Not *my* pa. No! I stamped my foot hard on a patch of ice and made loud cracking sounds. Jagged pieces scattered everywhere.

I kept walking, stamping ice patches—smashing those unspeakable thoughts, not even bothering to watch where I was going. I almost bumped right into Lila. She was rushing by, probably heading to the mail shack herself.

"Nothing today?" she asked, actually stopping in this bitter cold to hear my answer.

I hated her for asking. I turned and ran without giving her the satisfaction. I ran and ran not even noticing where I was going. But somehow my feet knew. They took me to the only place where I could warm myself all the way down to that deep aching place inside. I pushed the door open to a rush of sweet air.

"Fivel, my boy." Beryl always looked happy to see me. "What brings you here?" He patted the wooden stool. "Sit down." His big hand, covered with flour, left a soft powdery mark on the seat. I tried to smile but couldn't. *"Nu?"* So? he asked. "Why so sad?"

I shook my head and climbed onto the stool. Beryl didn't ask me anything else. I watched his large strong hands knead some dough. Push and fold. Push and fold. A comforting rhythm. For a while, I just sat there, slowly swinging my legs back and forth.

Finally, in a low whisper like a bad secret, I told him. "We didn't get anything from Pa."

"Well," he said, more like a breath than a real word and kept up the rhythm of his kneading. "There's always next time."

I nodded. But it didn't make the pain go away. And suddenly I knew why Ma and Hannah and Kvola gave each other those looks when I talked about all of us going to America. Even Benyomin would say, "Sure, sure," as if he didn't completely believe it anymore.

Now I asked Beryl urgently. "Do you think he will? Do you think he'll ever send us money?" That question hurt so much it burned my insides.

Beryl stopped kneading. "I wish I could tell you."

I nodded. I had another question—one that had been there as long as I could remember. No one could really answer it the way I wanted. But for some reason, I still liked to ask.

"What does my pa look like?"

Beryl smiled. "Like you, my Fivel. He's good-looking with thick dark hair." He gazed steadily, searching in his head for Pa. Then he turned back to me. "And he has kind brown eyes."

"Like yours," I said.

"Yes. Brown like mine." Beryl nodded.

"*Kind* like yours," I corrected.

Beryl smiled. "Your pa is lucky to have a son like you. I should only be so lucky. I'd keep you here forever." He shook his head. "But no, for your sake, I hope you get to America before things here get any worse."

CHAPTER 8

Each day pulled us deeper into winter. Pa and America were like tiny specks, drifting farther and farther away. I tried to keep believing we'd soon hear from Pa, but it was getting harder to convince myself.

Some days the only food I ate was at *heder* or at Beryl's. Without wanting to, I'd find myself thinking, *what if Beryl leaves for America?* Or, even worse, *what if Ma sends for that rich man and gives me away? One less mouth to feed.* Now, instead of wishing for America, I'd find myself hoping everything would just stay the same.

But then one day, our classmate Lahzer burst into *heder* shouting the thing that we all feared the most, "Cossacks are coming!"

Cossacks. Even the word terrified me.

Our teacher's face turned pale. He didn't question Lahzer. No one would make up such a thing. All he said was "Get home, all of you!" Benyomin jumped up, the first one out. I tried to follow. But I got caught in a rush for the door. Bigger boys shoved past, pushing me against the wall. I tried to force my way out, but they elbowed me back.

I was the last one out the door. I looked around. Benyomin was already gone. Probably halfway home by now. All the other boys were way ahead of me.

I ran to catch up. "Wait!" But of course they didn't. I soon lost sight of them.

My heart raced like wild horses. *Cossacks. Cossacks.* Alone on the road. Ma's words chased after me. *They kill little Jewish boys just for sport.* I ran so hard my lungs burned. My legs felt loose and wobbly. *Cossacks. Cossacks.* My feet pounded the frozen road, blocking out everything else.

I shot a glance behind me. The far hill was still empty. But any moment they'd come galloping over the top.

Ragged breaths seared my throat. Cossacks were the best swordsmen. So if they wanted to, they'd kill me in a flash. I ran with all my strength, not daring to look back again.

Benyomin must be home by now. So must all the other boys. Throughout the *shtetl,* doors were shut tight. I'd never seen it so quiet.

Ma's words echoed in my head. *Cossacks kill little Jewish boys. Kill little Jewish boys.* Her words snapped at my heels. *Just for sport. Just for sport.* Why did Benyomin leave me like this? Panting, panting, I kept going. Just a few more houses. Just a few more. *If there's talk of Cossacks, come right home.* And that's just what he'd done. I couldn't blame him. I'd have done the same if I'd had the chance.

At last, our house. I burst through the doorway, gasping. Ma, Hannah, and Kvola looked stricken with fear—as if I'd already been killed.

"Fivel!" Ma exclaimed. "Thank goodness you're safe!" She clutched me to her. "And, Benyomin," she gave him a sharp look. "Don't you ever go running ahead like that again. You make sure Fivel is with you."

"He was right behind me," Benyomin protested. "I didn't know he was so slow."

That hurt. I'd just run my hardest. My chest still ached. Slow! But I was panting too hard to speak.

Ma latched the door. "Go hide in the corner—all of you. Quick!"

Hannah and Kvola hurried us to the far wall. The four of us crouched down and huddled together on the hard dirt floor. My heart was still pounding, pounding. I squeezed close to Hannah. She drew her arm around me. Often when I needed a big sister, I turned to Kvola with her fiery spunk. But at times like this when I couldn't even stop shaking, I was glad for Hannah's soft, quiet comfort.

"Now stay right here," said Ma—more from fear than anything because none of us would dare move. She threw an old rug over us. "And *hush!*" As if she had to tell us! We were almost too frightened to breathe.

It was musty dark under there—except for a thin sliver of light coming through a long crack between the wooden slats of our house. Silently, we peered out. The road was still empty. Flat and lifeless. Maybe the Cossacks wouldn't come after all. Maybe it was just talk. But then, a dark smudge appeared over the far hill, then another and another charging forward.

To think I'd just been on that road! My heart lurched. They galloped toward our *shtetl. Ai,* were they big and fierce—handsome, too, in an icy way—with their tall fur hats, long swords, and thick bullet belts strapped across their chests.

If this was a *pogrom,* they'd break through our latched door in no time. Would they look under a dirty old rug heaped in the corner? And what about Ma? She was still at the stove stirring soup—to make it look like she was the only one home. *Please don't hurt her. Please.*

Pounding hooves filled my ears. They were so near I could see their dark mustaches and their pistols. I tucked myself closer to Hannah and shut my eyes.

But when I did, a terrible picture filled my head. It was from back when I was maybe five years old—a day I wished I could forget. Benyomin and I were playing behind Tomas and Ana's barn. Some Cossacks had been in the *pivne,* eating dark bread and drinking beer before their next battle somewhere. Suddenly we heard angry voices. We peeked around the corner. A few Cossacks were yelling at two young soldiers. They grabbed them by the shoulders and shook them fiercely.

"Spies!" they hissed and tore off the soldiers' caps.

To our amazement, long flowing hair tumbled out

and fell down the soldiers' backs. I gaped. There stood two beautiful young women probably just a few years older than Hannah and Kvola.

"Dirty spies!" The Cossacks spat at them and shoved them roughly against the wall. They drew their pistols.

It made no difference that they were young and beautiful. Before we could think, a deafening BANG filled our ears. They'd shot them both. If I'd known that would happen, I would have shut my eyes. But it was all too fast. They both slumped to the ground—dead.

Now, with my eyes closed tight, I saw it all again. Those two beautiful girls. Dead.

Benyomin grabbed my arm. "Such big horses!" he whispered.

I opened my eyes and peered out the crack. Cossacks on huge horses thundered past our house, kicking up clods of packed snow. From way ahead on the road, we heard guns shooting and cries of battle. They must be fighting other soldiers—probably near the long green bridge.

"Don't worry," said Kvola firmly. "Just let them keep fighting each other and leave us alone."

Yes, I thought. Stay away from us. No *pogrom.* I almost didn't dare think that word. But that's what we all feared. *Pogrom.* Cossacks tearing through the *shtetl,* ransacking houses and killing Jews.

When it was too dark to see, Ma took us all into bed

with her. We stayed there huddled together not knowing what would happen tomorrow.

The last time Cossacks had battled here, we'd stayed inside for days. I'd kept asking Ma why they were fighting and why we couldn't go out.

"It's too dangerous out there," she'd told me. "They're fighting to control our road, Ragotke Road."

"But why?"

"Because it's a main road."

But that didn't explain it any better.

"It's about who will control Poland," she went on. "Different armies pay the Cossacks to fight for them. The White Russians. The Red Russians. Those Cossacks don't care who they fight for as long as they get paid."

But that's not what worried me tonight. I huddled in bed between Ma and Hannah—thinking of the little latch on our door.

Mark my words, things will get worse for you Jews.

CHAPTER 9

The next morning, everything was quiet. We hoped that was a good sign. But we didn't dare go out. The Cossacks might still come back.

Bam! Bam! Bam! A heavy knock shook our door. My heart lurched. Ma shooed us over to the far wall and threw the rug over us again. *Bam! Bam! Bam!* My whole body shook.

"Come out!" BAM! BAM! BAM! "Come out! Benyomin! Fivel!" By the time I recognized the voice, my teeth were chattering.

I crawled out from under the rug. "Ma, it's Lahzer. Can I open the door?"

Ma nodded, pale with relief. I rushed over and unlatched it. There he stood grinning. He probably knew he'd scared us half to death. He'd probably wanted to. I didn't let on that he had. A group of boys from *heder*—just a little older than me—were crowding around him. "Come quick—or the big boys will get everything!" he urged. "Aren't you coming?"

"Are the Cossacks gone?" I was almost afraid to say it out loud.

"Klug!" Smart! exclaimed Lahzer. "Would we be out here otherwise? We've been up and down the *shtetl* already. Come on!"

I turned to Ma. She nodded that we could go. Benyomin and I hurried to join the boys. Lahzer led the way. The rest of us followed. I ran to keep up—in high spirits to be outside and safe after yesterday.

Today there'd be things worth finding, for sure. There always were after a battle. Warm clothes and who knew what else? Cossacks had the very best clothes of any of the soldiers.

"Tell me one good thing about a Cossack," we'd joke.

Someone would burst out, "His fur coat!" And we'd all laugh.

Then someone would say, "No, no. There's more than one good thing—his boots, his fur hat, his gloves . . ."

Suddenly we all stopped. There, lying on the roadside, was a dead Cossack. What luck! The big boys hadn't found him. He still had on all his winter clothes—his thick fur coat, his gloves and hat. Everything! I'd never gotten anything before this. But I was sure to get *something* today.

Right away, Lahzer and some others formed a tight circle around him. I tried to squeeze in. But they elbowed me out.

I shoved. But they wouldn't budge. I'd just have to wait for my chance.

There wasn't much time, though. Before long, the man

with the cart would come to haul the body away and toss it into a big hole. Whatever we wanted, we'd better take fast. Crouching low, I watched through their legs.

Of course the sword and pistol were gone. Some soldier must've gotten those. But everything else was still here.

I tried to squeeze through their legs. But they were holding tight.

Yonkel called out, "I get the gloves." He tugged one off, then the other, and waved them in the air.

"I get the coat!" cried Lahzer. He snatched an arm to claim it. Since he was the biggest, no one argued. "Shmuel, help me! Don't forget—I helped you last time."

That was true. Last time Shmuel had gotten the coat off a Red Russian soldier. Now he wore it all the time. It hung down to the ground. It wasn't as thick as this one. But it was warmer than anything the rest of us owned. Lahzer yanked at the arm of the Cossack's coat and pulled it free. They rolled the body over, and Lahzer tugged off the rest.

"Look." He pointed to a bullet hole in the coat. "He got shot right in the chest."

"He was a bad man," said Shmuel.

"They're all bad," said Lahzer. He quickly shoved his arms into the sleeves and pulled the coat on. Like Shmuel's, it hung to the ground. He'd be plenty warm. He searched the deep pockets. "A food bag!" he cried and dug into it pulling out a hunk of dark bread. We watched hungrily. He gave a good-sized piece to Shmuel. My stomach growled.

"Give us some," one boy demanded.

"Yeah!" I shouted. "We want some, too." We all moved in on him. Even though he was the biggest, he looked scared. He broke off a small piece for each of us. Mine was too small to cut through my hunger. Besides, it was frozen. I ate it slowly to make it last.

Benyomin gobbled his in no time. Then, while we were all still eating, he snatched the Cossack's tall fur hat and set it on his head. What a flash of luck. He marched around like a prince. *Ai!* Did I want that hat!

But oh! The boots were still there. Real leather. I reached over to grab them. Lucky me. I wouldn't need those leather scraps from the shoemaker after all. My heart raced. These were some handsome boots. *Ouch!* A boy shoved his elbow into my ribs.

"I get the boots!" he shouted.

"No! I get them," I cried. I *needed* those boots. My feet were so cold they ached. "I had them first!" I shouted at him.

"Did not!" He was already tugging them off the Cossack's feet. "You didn't even touch them." He was too big for me. I didn't have a chance. He kicked off his old worn shoes, pulled on the boots, and strutted around so everyone could see. By now, my feet were blocks of ice.

Benyomin pranced by me in his hat, showing off.

"Hey! Let me have a try." I grabbed at it.

"No!" He held on with both hands. "I only just got it."

"Money!" Shmuel cried. And we all turned to see. He pulled a fistful of coins from the Cossack's pants pocket. We only got a quick look before he tightened his fingers around the coins. This wasn't bread. We knew better than to even ask.

I looked down the road. The man with the cart was coming. No use hanging around. My feet were numb. And my fingers were aching stiff.

"I'm going home," I told Benyomin. I didn't need to watch him strutting around with that fur hat anymore. I trudged back through the *shtetl* alone, stamping my feet every few steps to get the feeling back in them. If only I was bigger, I would have gotten those boots for sure.

CHAPTER 10

I kept thinking how I'd come so close to getting those leather boots. Well, at least I could go see about the leather scraps at the shoemaker's. I'd managed to keep my secret all this time. It hadn't been easy.

One time, I did ask Hannah, "If I found some leather scraps, could you make me shoes?"

"Where would you find leather scraps?" she'd asked.

"Never mind where," I'd said. "Just could you make me shoes?"

"Don't go stealing anything," she'd warned. I'd promised I wouldn't, but she never did tell me if she could make me shoes. I knew she could, though. She could sew anything.

I was proud of myself for hanging onto my secret so long. It had been even harder holding off going back to the shoemaker's. Every day I'd think about it. Then I'd tell myself I had to wait and give him plenty of time to save enough scraps. Or else, he'd send me home with only a few *shtickel* pieces—not enough for shoes. So I held myself back. A big hopeful ache had grown inside me from all that waiting.

And now here I was looking in the window. There was a fine pair of men's boots on the shelf—just as shiny as those Cossack boots, maybe shinier. At least I could touch *these.* I'd feel how smooth and polished they were. And I'd get to warm myself up, too. My, that would feel good! I needed to tell myself all this just in case there weren't any scraps.

I pushed the door open and hurried in. The rich, sharp smell of leather filled my nostrils. It was so warm in there that my cheeks started to sting. I wiggled my toes to get them moving again.

"Git tog, little Fivel," Good day, the shoemaker greeted me in Yiddish and went back to sewing a leather sole on a shoe.

"Git tog." I ran my fingers lightly over the boots on the shelf. They were so smooth it made me shiver. "These are fine boots," I said.

His large, thick fingers kept working until he finished the sole. Then he reached under the counter. "Look here." He took out a small pair of shiny black boots. "What do you think of *these?*" He held them out for me to see.

A rush of longing swept through me. For some lucky rich boy! That's what I thought. I ran one finger along the tiny stitches. "So handsome!" I said, looking carefully so I could explain it all to Hannah—exactly how they were made. If only I could get those scraps. And this might be my best chance to ask.

"Last time I came," I began slowly, stroking the shiny black toe of one boot. "You said maybe you could find some scraps for me . . ."

"And you think I forgot?" The corners of his mouth twitched. "Look." He shook the boots at me. "I *did* find some."

What? My heart nearly smacked right through my ribs. But no. He must be joking. I searched his eyes. Did I dare ask? "For me?" I barely whispered, not even breathing.

The shoemaker nodded. "Yes, for you." He set them on the counter. "You like them?"

Like them? I grabbed them up and held them tightly against the crazy pounding in my chest. Even in my wildest dreams, I'd never imagined this. Shiny leather. Perfect stitches. These boots came from another world—a world I'd never put a single toe into.

"Try them on."

He didn't need to tell me twice. I kicked off my dirty, old wood shoes and slid my feet in. It was smooth as glass in there. I wiggled my toes. Plenty of room. Me and my feet were in heaven.

"They fit?" he asked.

"They're perfect." I nodded.

"Good." Now he really smiled—showing a few missing teeth. He shoved aside my old wood shoes with the tip of his boot. "You won't need these anymore. Now go and get some good wear out of those boots."

"I will!" I said. "Thank you!" I couldn't wait to get home and show Ma.

I ran so fast it felt like flying. I hoped Ma would be home. She'd be so surprised. They all would. Me with real leather boots.

I burst through the door. And, yes, Ma was there. "Look what the shoemaker made for me." I stood on a chair so everyone could admire them. Ma's eyes glistened.

Benyomin gave me a punch. "What makes you so lucky?" He was still wearing his Cossack hat. But that didn't bother me now.

Ma gave me a hug. *"Tsu reiss gezunterate!"* Tear them in good health.

"Tear them?" I made a face. "Never!"

She tousled my hair. "That's what we say. You should stay healthy and use them so much they wear out."

Not my leather boots, I thought. I planned to keep them shiny and new forever.

That night, I climbed onto the shelf above the oven—still in my boots. I fell asleep in them and dreamed about wearing them all the way to America.

In my dream, Pa looked so proud when he saw me in them. He lifted me up and swung me around. My boots whirled behind me. Pa's eyes glistened just like Ma's.

When I woke up, I still had that feeling inside me of being with Pa. But, hard as I tried, I couldn't remember his face.

CHAPTER 11

Winter held on for a long time. By now we longed for spring. Yet the hills stood cold and bare. Not a green speck on them. Finally the road turned thick with mud and slush. But then, everything froze again. Winter just wouldn't let go.

Warm or not, soon it would be *Pesach.* Passover. Ma worked at Beryl's helping bake *matzoh,* the unleavened bread for the holiday. Beryl kindly wrapped all the broken pieces in a large white cloth for Ma to take home. Benyomin and I were itching to try some. It seemed like half a lifetime ago—all the way back to last year—since we'd eaten any. We begged Ma for a taste. But she said no, we had to wait for *Pesach.* And just to make sure, she hung the cloth bundle from the ceiling by a nail to keep it safe. It hung there and hung there, just waiting for me to climb on a chair and make a little hole in the cloth—so little that no one would notice—and sneak a taste.

But the very next day Ma pointed to the hole. "What little mouse got into the *matzoh,* Fivel?" She gave me a raised eyebrow. I hoped she wasn't thinking what I was—*one less mouth to feed.* But then I saw a smile curling around her lips.

I lifted my eyes up to the ceiling and shrugged. "What little mouse?" After all, it had only been a taste or two. And Beryl had been so generous. If no one sneaked any more, it should last us through the holiday. And luckily, even with those few little tastes missing, it did.

After Passover, after the last crumb of *matzoh* was gone, it was still too cold out to believe that winter was over. Spring trickled slowly in. It seemed like forever before the ground grew soft and warm again. Finally the mountains on either side of the *shtetl* turned green. At last, we'd made it through winter.

I wanted to thumb my nose at the rich man in those city clothes. "See?" I wanted to tell him. "Ma didn't need you. See?" But in my mind, he was still there, smug as ever, *Mark my words, things will get worse.*

"No!" I'd shout at him in my head, "You're wrong." But then I'd notice Ma's worry lines. They etched her forehead so often now, almost part of her normal face. Lately we'd heard there'd been a *pogrom* nearby. But thank goodness our *shtetl* had been spared. "See?" I'd argue with him. "Ma doesn't need you."

"Look, Fivel," Benyomin cut into my thoughts one morning and opened the door, letting in the warm sun. "It's not even cold out today. You don't have to wear your stupid boots anymore."

Not wear my boots? He must be joking. I always wore

them, even to bed. I strutted around the table. Beryl had told me they were the finest boots he'd ever seen on a boy—even in Vilna. People were always admiring them.

"Come on," urged Benyomin. "Take off those stupid boots already."

"No." I galloped around the table. "Never!"

"You're *meshuggeneh.* Crazy." Benyomin set his fur hat on his head. "Let's go out."

"What about your stupid hat? It's not even cold out." I tried to grab it. But he ducked out of reach. "Take it off," I teased.

Benyomin grinned. "Never!" He strutted by me. I snatched at it and this time I got it.

"Ha!" I set it on my head and ran straight for the door. But I didn't get far. He grabbed it back before I was halfway there.

"You boys!" Ma scolded. But she was smiling. The worry lines smoothed out for a moment. It was a good day. Kvola had earned some extra money cleaning houses. And now Ma was baking dark rolls. She set the mounds of dough on some big leaves she'd gathered and slid them into the oven. "Go outside and play. Wear your boots and hat if you like. Just remember, don't go far. In case . . ." We knew what she was thinking. Cossacks. She gave us each a gentle swat on the backside. "And stay together."

"We will," Benyomin promised, as he ran outside barefoot with his fur hat on.

"Don't worry, Ma," I called over my shoulder as I hurried after him in my boots. Poor Ma, always worried about Cossacks and *pogroms*—even on a beautiful day like this when the sky was so blue and wide open it seemed nothing could go wrong.

"Let's go see Beryl," I suggested. Now that it was warmer out, I liked helping him with his chickens. And sometimes he gave me an egg or two. If we were lucky, I even got a couple extra for hatching.

Benyomin dug a toe in the dirt. "No. Let's play with the wheel." This was nothing new. We'd played with that wheel almost every day since the snow had melted. I hated to admit it, but he was much better than me—probably because his legs were longer or maybe because he worked at it all the time. When he got going, it was as if the whole world fell away and nothing else mattered.

"How about let's go next door and play with Yusig." I grinned at the thought.

"Good idea!" Benyomin leaped in the air. We hadn't done that in the longest time—since way back in the fall when I'd been so worried about Mira finding out. By now that worry seemed foolish and far away.

We ran around getting everything all set—the flat wood pieces, the horse dung. We made it look perfect. Then we knocked on Yusig's door. Mira came and opened it. I'd hardly seen her all winter. She looked even more beautiful than I remembered.

"Yusig's not here right now," she told us in Polish.

I stood there gazing at her, trying to draw out the time as long as I could—enjoying the soft, creamy look of her cheeks and her long, shiny brown hair. Finally I said, "Please tell him we came by."

"I will." She smiled and closed the door.

As we left, Benyomin held my arm so I had to stop. "You were gaping at her like *this*." He let his mouth hang wide open and his eyes bug out big and stupid looking.

The blood rushed to my cheeks. "Was not!" I gave him a shove. "Anyway, she smiled at *me*—not you," I pointed out.

"She was laughing at you," he teased. "You're in love. And she's as old as Hannah. She's way too old for you, Fivel."

I tried to punch him, but he ran away laughing. Of course he was right. And that made it even worse.

"I get the wheel first!" He dashed for it. It was leaning against our house with the long stick we always used. He grabbed the stick, tapped the wheel, and had it rolling in no time. He was still laughing as he raced down the dirt road.

I ran after him. He dashed along with that wheel, fast and smooth, making it look so easy. It seemed he barely even tapped it. The wheel almost rolled on its own—with him flying along behind. This must be the longest he'd ever kept it up. And he was still going. Oh, would he be bragging! That made me run harder. I charged forward and jostled into him.

The wheel fell.

"Oops." I laughed. "Sorry!"

"No fair!" He threw down the stick. "You did that on purpose."

I laughed again and grabbed the wheel. "You had it too long anyway. It's my turn now." I snatched the stick and headed off.

But he caught up in no time. "It's still my turn." He tugged the stick out of my hand and grabbed the wheel. He was off again. It would be a long time now before I got another turn.

Well, I'd show him. "I'm going to Beryl's!" I called after him and started down the path. Already I was thinking how Beryl might have a couple extra hatching eggs for me. Ma would be so pleased. We'd put them under the clay oven to keep warm. Being the smallest, I could still get under there easily. When they hatched, I'd take care of them. And when they were big enough, mmmm. My mouth watered at the thought of eating chicken. I quickened my step, heading straight for the bakery—not once looking back.

CHAPTER 12

Beryl was in his fenced yard. A mass of busy chickens clucked around him.

"Shalom aleichem!" Hello to you. He waved.

"Aleichem shalom." And to you. I slid through the gate and hurried to the feed sack. Digging my hand in, I tossed feed all around. The chickens bobbed and pecked at the ground—a whirl of clucking feathers. Beryl and I laughed. Everything felt good and right with the world. The whole day seemed to be smiling.

Then, as if from nowhere, came a burst of pounding feet. Village boys raced by without stopping. "Cossacks are coming!" they shouted. I shot a look at the far hills. None were in sight. But already my heart was jumping.

"Go home, Fivel," Beryl called as he swung his big arms, shooing the chickens into the coop. "Hurry!" He kept shooing. Cossacks would surely grab any that were left in clear view.

"I need to get Benyomin," I cried. "He's on the road."

"There's no time," Beryl shouted. "He knows the way home. Now go!"

I stood there unsure what to do. Ma had told us to stay together. I was the one who'd left.

"Go home!" Beryl ordered. "Run!" His voice was so sharp it made me jump.

I dashed out the gate. Benyomin must've heard those boys yelling. He must be running home. He might even be ahead of me by now. "Benyomin!" I called as I raced toward home, glancing down each path along the way.

Everywhere people were rushing into their houses, latching the doors behind them. I ran through our *shtetl* calling, "Benyomin!" My heart knocked against my ribs.

Shmuel ran past me. He pointed in the direction of the hills. "He's way back there with the wheel!"

Back there? His words gripped me by the chest. Without a second thought, I turned and ran toward the hills hard and fast.

Past Beryl's—not one chicken left in the yard. Past house after house. Past the very last one. Everything seemed strangely quiet. The only sounds came from my boots pounding the road and my own gasping breath.

The road dipped and climbed. Why had I left him? Why? Ma had told us to stay together. Now only steep mountains towered on either side of me. No one was in sight. In this eerie quiet, I felt very small.

My heart banged its own warning. *Get home. Get home.* But I sped along, panting.

The road dipped again. And there he was way down at the bottom of the hill, with that stupid wheel, tapping it with the stick and racing along as if nothing else mattered.

"Benyomin!" I shouted so hard my throat almost ripped wide open. But he kept right on going. "Benyomin!" I screamed loud enough to wake the dead. But the wind snatched my words away. "Cossacks!" My voice sounded strange and shrill. "Get home!" I shrieked.

Finally he looked my way. "They're coming!" I pointed wildly up the road. "Run!"

Then I ran. He'd overtake me in no time. I'd be last on the road again—with Cossacks at my heels. My heart thundered like horses' hooves. I ran harder than ever until the road, my boots, and my hurting breath all pounded in one urgent beat. *Home. Home.*

I raced past house after house. Doors were shut tight. I ran like a scared rabbit.

Ma would be so worried by now. But I'd gotten Benyomin. That's all that mattered.

Our little rundown house never looked so good. Breathless, I charged inside.

"Thank goodness you're safe!" Ma held me close. "Where's Benyomin?"

"He's coming." I panted.

There was a quick knock on the door. "That must be him." I pulled it open.

But it was Ana from next door. Her face was gray with fear. "It looks bad this time," she told Ma. "Many Cossacks are already over the far hill." She shot a look around to make sure no one was watching. Then from her sleeve she pulled out a small silver cross and pressed it into Ma's hand. "Put this on your door. Then it will look like a Christian home. The Cossacks will leave you alone."

"You and Tomas are good neighbors," said Ma.

"You are the same," said Ana, glancing over her shoulder again. "Your boys are always kind to my Yusig." That made me wince. "Nothing should happen to any of you." And she hurried home.

"Or any of you," Ma called after her. With trembling hands she hung the cross on the door. It looked strange there. Benyomin would surely joke about it when he saw it.

Why wasn't he here already? He'd looked straight at me when I'd yelled *Cossacks*. He must have heard.

"Where can he be?" Ma shot an anxious look down the road. She stepped outside, arms wrapped tightly around herself. Her eyes searched both directions. Deep worry lines creased her forehead. "You all stay here," she said sternly. "I'll find him." And before we could think, she'd rushed off.

"Don't go far, Ma," I called after her. "He'll be home in no time."

"Be careful," Kvola warned—although Ma was already gone. She closed the door slowly, not shutting it all the way. We looked at each other, without a word. Better not to speak our fears.

Hannah was already at the back wall peering out.

"Can you see Ma or Benyomin?" I asked.

"Oh no!" she shrieked. "No!" She covered her face and burst into tears.

"What? What?!" Kvola and I rushed over. I peered through the crack. Ma was nowhere in sight. But far down the road was one small boy. Too small to be Benyomin, I told myself. But he wore a fur hat and was running with a wheel.

Suddenly he looked over his shoulder and froze. Cossacks were thundering toward him. He dropped the wheel and ran.

The door burst open letting in a raw chill. We all jumped. "I can't find him," Ma gasped. "I went up and down everywhere. He must be in someone's house."

"Oh, Ma!" Hannah threw herself into Ma's arms sobbing.

"What?" screamed Ma. "Tell me!"

"He's still on the road." Kvola flung her arm at the back wall.

The color drained from Ma's face. "No!" She dashed over and peered out the crack. "Benyomin!" she shrieked as if someone had stabbed her. "Oh! Heaven help him!" She rushed for the door.

Kvola grabbed her arm. "No! You'll get killed."

"I have to!" Ma cried fiercely, yanking free.

"He's too far." Hannah's face crumpled. "You won't make it."

"Please, Ma." I grabbed hold of her arm. "Please don't go!" I broke into sobs. But she wrenched herself away.

CHAPTER 13

Kvola stood firmly, arms outstretched, blocking the door. "You'll never reach him, Ma. You'll only get killed." She seemed so strong and sure of herself, as she quickly latched the door. But when she turned back to face Ma, her shoulders slumped. She gave Ma a helpless, pleading look.

Ma didn't say a word. She sank down by the back wall, heavy as a stone, and peered through the long crack. We all joined her there, holding on to each other. Kvola draped the rug over us. I wanted to shut my eyes. But I needed to see my brother.

Benyomin raced down the road. Cossacks galloped toward him.

"Run, Benyomin, run." I squeezed Ma's hand. "He's fast. He'll make it." He just had to reach a house—any house.

We all watched, gripping each other. "Hurry, Benyomin!" In my mind, I was right at his heels, urging him faster. He'd almost reached the house way at the end of the *shtetl*. I squeezed my fists together. "Run, Benyomin!"

He threw himself at the door of that house and pounded.

"He made it!" I cried with relief. "He's safe!" But the door did not open.

"Someone open the door!" I shouted.

Benyomin kept pounding. But no one came. He looked over his shoulder. Cossacks thundered closer. He ran to the next house and pounded.

"Open up!" I cried. But no one came. He ran to the next house and the next. He pounded and pounded. Door after door. No one came.

"They're too afraid," said Kvola grimly. "If they open the door, those Cossacks could charge in."

I knew that fear. And I hated it.

"Oh heaven help him!" Ma wailed.

Now the leader pointed his sword at Benyomin and shouted something to the Cossack behind him. I tried to pull my eyes away but couldn't. The other Cossack drew his sword, spurred his horse, and charged.

"No!" I cried. But the Cossack slashed the sword right at Benyomin's head. I clenched my jaw and shut my eyes tight. From Ma came a wrenching sound like from a wounded animal. But then came a softer cry of amazement.

I opened my eyes a tiny bit. By now the sky was dim. But I thought I saw . . . was it possible? Benyomin, still standing. Yes! And there was his fur hat swinging from the point of the sword. The Cossack tilted the sword straight up and raised the hat high in the air like a prize. He yelled something to the leader, threw back his head, and laughed.

With that, they let out blood-raging shouts and charged forward. In a blur, Cossacks and horses filled the road where Benyomin stood.

By now it was so dark out, I could barely see. Was that Benyomin on the ground? That small unmoving heap? Wordless fear lodged in the pit of my stomach. Every muscle in my body wanted to run out and grab him. But I knew I'd just be killed. It was all darkness and shadows out there now.

For that one moment, everything had seemed so hopeful. I'd really believed that maybe they'd let him live. Just a boy. Not hurting anyone. But it was only sport for them—swiping his hat. They didn't care about my brother. They'd trampled right over him. I shook my head hard, trying to shake away the truth. Ma's face was lifeless. Her shoulders hung limply.

"We should eat," said Kvola without any spirit. She brought us the rolls Ma had baked this morning. Had it really been only this morning? It seemed like an altogether different time since Benyomin and I had run out laughing. And Ma had told us to stay together. It had been so warm and sunny back then. Now a cutting chill had set in. *If only I'd stayed with him.*

None of us felt like eating. I shivered. It was cold out there. And pitch dark.

"He was a good boy," Ma said softly—sort of pleading. "Such a good boy."

Without meaning to, I found myself selfishly wondering if she would say that about me if I ever got killed. I curled close against her.

The sounds outside were terrible. Doors smashing. People screaming. I thought of Ana's little cross on our door. To keep us safe. But what about Benyomin? Every sound out there made me jump. We huddled under the rug. Kvola brought a hot stone from the oven to keep us warm. But nothing could warm the icy chill inside me.

CHAPTER 14

All the next day Cossacks stormed our *shtetl.* We stayed under the rug by the back wall and watched what little we could through the slats. They were bashing down doors and crashing into homes carrying off anything they wanted—brass candlesticks, silver *Kiddush* cups, anything valuable. Rocking softly, Ma whispered the Hebrew prayers. Silently I said my own prayers. *Please make him safe. Please make us safe.* One time we heard gunshots and terrible screams very close by. The sounds sent a death chill through me. They seemed to come from Ana's house. But no, that wasn't possible. Their family had a big silver cross on their door.

We stayed hidden inside and said very little, only what was needed. Nothing about Benyomin. Nothing about the *pogrom,* this endless nightmare.

An unbearable emptiness hung around us. Would we find his body? All trampled? Would we even be able to recognize him?

The next day, the Cossacks thundered past our house on their big horses. Then everything was unusually quiet. It seemed they were gone. Still, we didn't dare go out. We waited more than half the day.

Finally Ma opened our door and lifted off the little silver cross. "I must check on them," she said and hurried to Ana's house. When she came back, her face was pale as ashes. "I have terrible news." She sank into a chair as if her body was too much for her. "Ana, Tomas . . ." Her hands fell into her lap. She picked mindlessly at her apron and shook her head. "The whole family. They're all dead."

"No!" Kvola covered her face. "No!"

"It can't be," Hannah pleaded. "They had that big cross on their door."

"But they were rich." Ma narrowed her eyes. "Those rotten Cossacks ransacked the whole place—the house, the barn, everything."

All I could think of was beautiful Mira.

"I can't believe it." Ma let out a heavy sigh. "They were such good people. They saved our lives."

It made me shiver. Mira. How could they kill her? Beautiful Mira. I felt sick to my stomach. And Ana. She was so kind to us. And Yusig. With stinging guilt I thought of the trap we'd made for him just the other day. Me and Benyomin.

We'd heard the screams next door. But none of us had said our fear aloud—just as none of us were saying it now about Benyomin.

With grim faces, all of us headed out to the spot where we'd last seen him. But there was nothing—no sign of him at all. We trudged through the *shtetl*—even Hannah—asking everyone we saw. "Did you see Benyomin—the little Jewish boy? He was outside when the Cossacks came." "Did you see his body somewhere?" "Do you know what happened to him?"

No one did.

I even went to Lila's house. I hated to. But if anyone would know, she would. "Do you know what happened to Benyomin?" I asked.

"No. What?" She leaned in sucking her breath. "Tell me." She gripped my shoulder.

"We don't know," I said shaking her off. I quickly left before she could ask anything else. I hated her for not knowing. And I hated her even more for wanting to know.

No one knew. Numbness filled the *shtetl* like thick fog. Wherever we went, people were in shock. Bad news followed us everywhere. This one dead. That one dead. But no one knew anything about Benyomin.

Maybe the Cossacks had carried him off and left him somewhere. We searched the road and ditches, dreading what we'd find. Beryl went out with his horse and wagon far beyond our *shtetl* in both directions but didn't find a trace. Ma never scolded me for not staying with Benyomin that day. No one mentioned it. But I couldn't stop thinking—if only I *had*.

Why hadn't I made sure he'd heard me when I ran

back to get him? That question tortured me. What kind of brother was I? So afraid to be the last one on the road? Or still mad that he'd teased me about Mira? Or that he was so much better than me with that wheel? Such small stupid things. Nothing made sense. I should have run all the way there and grabbed him.

I pictured it a hundred times in my head—just how I should have done it. Again and again I asked myself, What kind of brother was I?

Beryl seemed to know what I was thinking. He put his arm around my shoulders and gave a squeeze. "Don't blame yourself. You thought Benyomin heard you. There's nothing else to it. You did the right thing or else you'd also be . . ." He shook his head and didn't say it.

I wanted to believe Beryl—that I'd done the right thing. But I knew I should have stayed with Benyomin or, at least, gone all the way there and grabbed him. It left me gasping inside—as if I were running the same race over and over. Each time I ran my hardest and each time I lost.

That evening, tired and worn out, I crawled up to the shelf above the oven. It was empty as death. I tightened into a ball, squeezing back the tears. I tried to fall asleep. But I kept seeing Benyomin running off with that wheel. I should have stayed with him. If only I had!

I would've heard all the yelling about Cossacks coming. I would've grabbed him. We'd have run home together, safe—with plenty of time.

If only, if only.

There was a knock on the door.

Ma got up heavily and unlatched it. She opened it a crack and gasped. And then, like some waiting prayer, Ma said the one word that my whole body was aching for: "Benyomin!"

I hardly believed my ears. I leaped down in no time. And yes, there he was—already in Ma's arms.

"Benyomin. Oh, my Benyomin!" she said over and over, tears streaming down her face. Hannah and Kvola were sobbing and laughing all at once. I hopped from one foot to the other, too excited to stand still.

"Benyomin!" Oh it felt good to say his name! "Tell us," I urged. "What happened?"

But Kvola jumped in. "We saw that Cossack swipe your hat. And then . . . ooh!" She shivered. "We thought you got trampled. So tell us, Benyomin!"

"Give him a minute to catch his breath," said Ma, wiping her tears away. "He'll tell. Don't worry. He's not going anywhere!" And that was the sweetest truth.

"That hat saved my life," Benyomin said. He finally took a chair. Ma lit a spindle of wood. And we all sat down around him. "That Cossack would have killed me for sure. But the leader dared him to just get my hat. You all saw? He missed my head by *that* much." He showed with his fingers how close.

I shuddered.

"Then I got knocked down. See?" He showed us big bruises on his back. Dark purple and green.

I winced. "That hurts!"

Benyomin nodded. "I would've gotten trampled. But I rolled off the road." He gulped a breath and went on. "An old lady opened her door a crack and motioned me in."

"What a brave woman!" Ma exclaimed.

"I flew in there so fast." His eyes grew wide. "She latched the door and told me I had to stay until they were all gone. She even fed me!" He patted his stomach and licked his lips. "But she wouldn't let me leave." He shrugged. "Even this afternoon, when everything was quiet, she was afraid they might come back. She worried what would happen if she opened her door. But finally when it got dark, she let me go home."

"I can never thank her enough," said Ma. "Never."

That night, I gave Benyomin all the room he wanted on the shelf, gladly. But there was still something bothering me. "Why didn't you come home when I called you?"

"You called me to come *home?*" Benyomin sounded puzzled. "Way down the road? When I had the wheel?"

"Yes," I answered.

"How can that be?" he said almost to himself. "I thought you said, *It's my turn or I'm going home.*"

"What?" I snorted. "You thought I ran all that way for a stupid wheel?" I burst out laughing. It was so dumb. I couldn't stop.

But Benyomin wasn't laughing. He was quiet for a while. Then softly, he said, "You ran all the way back to get me?"

"Of course, you numskull."

"And you knew that Cossacks were coming?"

"That's why I went! I thought you heard me for sure. So then I ran home." And finally I knew, in the truest corner of my heart, that this was so.

He gave my arm a squeeze. "You're some brother." That's all he said. But that was plenty.

I fell right to sleep thinking the worst was over.

CHAPTER 15

For days after, I barely let Benyomin out of my sight. Even if he went to the outhouse, I went along and waited right outside, glad to be nearby—smell and all!

We never went far from home anymore. And we didn't play by Ana's house either. It seemed too much like a sad dark hole. We still played with the wheel a lot. But we only ran along the road a short ways. I was getting pretty good at it. Of course Benyomin was still better. But as far as I was concerned, he could be as good as he wanted.

One day we were outside playing with the wheel. It was Benyomin's turn, and I was running alongside. Suddenly he stopped short, hardly even noticing that the wheel had dropped.

"Fivel!" He grabbed my arm and tugged me so close I could feel his chest heaving. Each breath came out short and fast. "Look!" He pointed with his finger tight against his body.

A fine-looking horse and carriage had stopped in front of Tomas and Ana's house. A well-dressed man stepped out.

Yanking me even closer, Benyomin whispered in my ear, "That's the man who wants to take you."

My throat tightened. I stared at the man and tried to fit him with the one in my head. "No." I shook my head firmly. "The other man was bigger."

"No, he wasn't. That's him!" Benyomin insisted. "I remember his horse and carriage. I remember his mean face."

I looked at the man carefully—the trim mustache, the thin lips, the long, deep frown lines curving down from his mouth. This did look awfully like him. But it was as if he suddenly shrank.

"It's him all right," said Benyomin. And I had to agree that something about him was unmistakable—the way he carried himself like he was so important, the way he sort of sniffed down his nose at people going by on the road.

All these months, he must've been growing in my head. And now here he was no bigger than any ordinary man. But he looked as mean as ever.

Benyomin and I inched backwards—slowly, so as not to draw attention to ourselves. He was heading right toward our house.

What should I do? Run inside and beg Ma? *Please don't give me away. Please.*

Or should I run and hide? That's what my whole body was screaming. *Run and hide. Run and hide.*

But no. Then Ma would be angry with me and have even more reason to give me away.

Why now, though? We'd made it all the way through winter. We'd survived the *pogrom*. Why had she sent for him now? Was it too hard to feed us all? Was I eating too much? More than my share?

I'd promise to eat less. I'd *promise*.

A plan was forming in my head. The man mustn't reach our house. He mustn't speak to Ma.

"I'm stopping him," I said and lurched forward.

Benyomin pulled me back. "Are you crazy?"

But I tugged free, my heart nearly busting out of my chest. I had to keep the man away from Ma. I ran so fast that I knocked right into him.

"Uh!" He pinched his mouth together and brushed himself off.

"Excuse me, sir." I stepped back.

He gave a sniff and started walking toward our house again.

I hurried alongside—trying to think of what to say. "I'm Mrs. Myzel's boy," I blurted out. "And Ma says we're doing much better now. She says I don't need to go with you."

He stopped and looked down at me. "Is that so?"

"Yes. I even have these new leather boots. See?" I showed him.

"I see," he said, but his eyes were on my torn pants,

not my boots—which still looked new and shiny in my head. But when I really looked, I saw they were scuffed and worn. "Here," he offered me a candy wrapped in shiny paper. Once Beryl had brought me one like that from Vilna. My mouth watered. "Go ahead. Take it." He shook it at me impatiently. "I need to speak to your mother."

"No thank you." I held my hands tightly behind me so they wouldn't do what I didn't want them to. He shrugged, put the candy back into his pocket, and started toward our house again.

"Wait, sir," I called, not knowing what to say, only knowing I must stop him. "I'm not a good boy. Your wife wouldn't want me."

He looked down at me and stroked his nose with his pointer finger. "Is that so?"

"Yes. You should find someone else for her."

"I'll decide that for myself." He sniffed. "Now I need to talk to your mother."

"I *won't* go with you," I shouted out. "I'm *not* a good boy." I stood in front of him blocking the way.

"I see!" he spoke sharply. "I see that's quite true. A good boy would not think only of himself. He'd think of his family." He gave me a look that cut right into me. "He'd want to help them if he had the chance."

Oh, I hated him! But what he said was true. Poor Ma. Always worried about food. Now there'd be one less mouth to feed. Now my family would have more to eat.

"I must speak with your mother." He pushed me aside and walked up the path, his face set with those dark frown lines. It sent quivers through me. How could I ever go with such a man? I'd miss Ma something awful. Tears filled my eyes. I'd miss everyone.

By now, he was at our door. He gave a sharp knock. In no time, Ma opened it.

"Good afternoon, Mrs. Myzel." His mouth formed a stiff smile—showing all his teeth. "I was just talking to your little boy here. He told me you are doing much better." He lifted both eyebrows in a question. Ma shot a quick look at me and then turned back to the man. I hoped with all my heart she wasn't angry at me for saying that. "But . . ." the man went on. "It seems that you are still doing rather poorly. And I want to help you. My offer still holds. I will gladly take the boy."

I wanted to throw myself at Ma and beg her, "Please don't make me go. *Please.*" But I forced myself to say, "I'll go, Ma. If you want me to." I nearly choked into tears. But I held them back and worked hard to think about all the extra food they'd have without me.

"He'll have a good home," the man went on. And I desperately hoped he was telling the truth. "He'll have everything that you can't give him—a far better life than this." He threw a disgusted look around our house. "I'm sure you'll agree it's the wisest thing to do."

Ma's face stiffened. "No," she said as clearly as any word I'd ever heard in my life. "My son is right. We don't need your help."

My heart almost stopped beating. I could have melted right into the ground I was so weak with relief.

"Hmph!" He sniffed. "You are a foolish woman."

Ma gave him a hard angry look but kept her mouth closed tight.

The man glared back at her. "Perhaps you will recognize the wisdom of my offer and change your mind before it's too late." He stuck his chin up and sniffed again. "For now, I must be gone. Good day." He strode quickly back to his carriage.

As soon as he was safely away, I ran to Ma and threw my arms around her. "Thank you, Ma!"

She frowned at me. "Don't be foolish, Fivel. That's not worth a thank you. You're my son."

"But what about that paper he gave you?" I drew in a shaky breath. "Are you still keeping it—in case you change your mind?" My voice was thin and quivery, but finally, I'd asked.

"What paper?" Ma shook her head. "He didn't give me any paper. I don't know what you're talking about."

"Oh, *I* know what he means," Kvola spoke up. "Don't you remember, Ma? Last time he was here that man gave you a paper with his name and address. You put it right where it belonged that very same day." She nodded firmly. "Into the fire."

"You did?" I looked up at Ma and rubbed my runny nose with the back of my hand. "So you didn't send for him?"

"*Send* for him?" Ma gazed at me with a sudden softness in her eyes. "Fivel, did you really think I might give you away?"

"Yes." A sob tore out of me.

"Oh, my Fivel." Ma gently stroked my head. "I'd never do that. It hurts too much. Believe me. I know." She lifted my face and looked straight into my eyes. "I'd rather starve. Do you hear me, Fivel?"

A thin trickle of tears crept down the sides of my nose. "Yes, Ma. I do."

CHAPTER 16

After that, Benyomin and I played with the wheel just like always—nothing different, but for me, everything was different. My whole world was sunnier than it had been for the longest time. Benyomin was still better at the wheel. But I was taking good long turns nowadays, too.

One day, on one of my longer turns, the mail wagon drew into view. I stopped short, not caring at all that the wheel had dropped. "Look, Benyomin! Come on." I pulled his sleeve. "Let's go!" We'd been staying so close together lately, I was sure he'd come.

But he waved me on. "No. You go."

"Please?" I hated leaving him for anything—even this. "Just this once?" He looked as if he might come so I added, "I have *such* a good feeling today."

But that didn't work how I'd hoped. He frowned. "You always say that. And there's never anything for us. You should know by now. But go ahead with your good feeling. I'll just take my turn." He grabbed the wheel and started running with it.

"Don't go far," I called after him—even though I knew he wouldn't.

Ma was baking bread. Soon it would be out of the oven. Hot and fresh. We both wanted to be there. So no matter what happens at the mail shack, I told myself, with bread in the oven, it's still a good day. And I still have a good feeling.

"See you soon," I shouted and raced off.

My heart galloped the whole way and almost beat me there. By now, the mail wagon was pulling away. As always, tingles swept through me when I walked through the doorway and up to the counter.

"Do you have anything for the Myzels?" I asked.

For once, the man behind the counter took a real look without my even asking. That alone made me grateful. He rummaged around, and then, I could hardly believe my eyes, set a package down in front of me.

I gaped in disbelief. "For the Myzels?"

"That's what it says." He pointed to the writing on the package. *"The Myzels. Ragotke Road. Vilkomerski: Poland.* Is that your family?"

"Yes." My heart was dancing like crazy.

"Here." He pushed it toward me. "It's from America."

"From America!" What a delicious sound that made in my mouth! "Thank you!" I clutched it to me and hurried out, running through the *shtetl* in great flying leaps.

Benyomin came racing up. "What? We got a package?"

"Yes! And *I'm* giving it to Ma."

"Just let me see it for a second." He reached for it.

But I held on tight and ran for all I was worth.

I tore into the house shouting, "Look Ma! Look what we got!"

Ma, Hannah, and Kvola rushed over. Benyomin dashed in right behind me. With everyone watching, I proudly handed the package to Ma.

She held it as if it were something holy. I hugged myself. Our house smelled so good with Ma's bread just out of the oven. We watched as she carefully, almost tenderly, removed the brown paper wrapping, then the stiff cardboard, and then more brown paper. We barely breathed as she lifted off the last piece of paper and uncovered a large wooden picture frame. There under the glass, was a black and white photograph. A man with soft, kind eyes.

"Look! It's Pa!" exclaimed Kvola.

Hannah sucked in a breath.

Pa. I gazed, unable to get enough.

"Let me see." Benyomin bent close to the frame.

"He's so handsome!" I looked up eagerly at Ma.

But, strangely, she did not seem happy. She shook her head—not hiding her disappointment.

"A picture?" Her voice took on a harsh edge. "After all this time—a worthless picture! In a wooden frame, no less!" Her face turned hard. "He thinks so much of himself? Uh! Such a waste of money!" Her voice rose. "Why?!" A big blue vein on her neck bulged out. "Why would he do this to us?" Tears welled in her eyes, but she rubbed them angrily away. "Of all things!" Her voice grew hateful. "We're *starving!*" She screamed at Pa's picture. "Are you *meshuggeneh*? We can't eat a picture!" she shrieked. I'd never seen her so upset. It was as if all the years of waiting and never hearing, all that was exploding out of her.

"But Ma," I said softly. "Don't you see . . . ?" I tried to explain how it was for me, "Now I know his face. I know my pa." I gently touched his cheek. My handsome pa.

"It's a worthless picture!" Ma screamed. "Worthless!" She snatched it off the table and before any of us could stop her, she strode over to the oven and shoved it into the fire.

"No!" I cried. "You can't do that!" I'd never said such a thing to Ma before. But a big aching piece of me was in there with it. "I need it!" I rushed over and, not even thinking, plunged my hand in and wrenched it out.

The picture was already in flames. I dropped it on the floor. Glass shattered everywhere. Flames curled around the edges of Pa's face. Heart pounding, I stamped them out with my boots.

"I *need* his picture," I said more firmly than I'd ever said anything to Ma, tears spilling down my face. "I *need* it." I held my burnt fingers to my mouth and leaned down close, wiping my eyes to see what was left. The edges of the picture were singed and crumbling. But his soft, kind eyes and his handsome face were still there.

And what was this showing from under the singed

edges? Something green. With raw, burnt fingers, and pounding heart, I carefully, carefully lifted Pa's picture and set it on the table. And there, showing plainly, as if it had floated straight out of my dreams and onto our hard dirt floor, was money—money from America—more than we'd ever seen.

For a few seconds we stared, stunned. Pa had held all of this in his own hands. He'd hidden it safely—just as I'd always hoped. And now, with trembling fingers, I scooped it up and handed it to Ma, still warm.

Ma's lips quivered. With tears in her eyes, she looked at me with such a mixture of shame and pride. "I can't believe it!" She held the money in both hands and burst into sobs.

But we children believed it. We jumped up and down hugging each other and shouting, "Pa sent money! Pa sent MONEY!"

"Shh!" Ma quickly shoved all of it into her straw mattress. "We mustn't tell anyone. Someone could steal it." Her face stiffened. "We don't know who we can trust."

"Well *I* know who," I said with certainty. "We can trust Beryl. Always."

Ma's face smoothed with relief. *"Ah lebmeh dine kuppaleh."* A blessing on your head. She patted my head. "Go right now, Fivel. Tell him I'll come by soon. Maybe he'll know what it's worth. Who knows? Maybe it's enough to get us to—" She stopped, not daring to say it aloud. But nothing could stop me. Already, my heart was singing it over and over. *America. America. America.*

I headed straight to Beryl's, gulping in great breaths of air.

Halfway there, Lila rushed up to me. "Fivel!" She caught me by the elbow. "*Nu?* You got a package?"

"Yes—from Pa!" I exclaimed and yanked my arm free. "He sent us a picture of himself!" And I ran off as fast as I could, laughing out loud.

"Beryl!" I shouted as I rushed in the bakery. "Pa sent us money!"

"What? He did?"

"Yes. And *I* found it! It was hidden inside a wooden picture frame." I jumped up and down. "Ma threw it into the oven. But I grabbed it out just in time."

"Thank goodness!" he exclaimed.

"It's this much." I showed him, holding a thick space between my thumb and pointer finger.

"*Ai, yai, yai!*" Beryl rocked his head back and forth. "It must be a fortune!"

"Yes," I agreed. "Ma will come soon. She needs to know if it's enough to get us to America. You'll help us, won't you?"

"What a question!" Beryl threw his hands in the air. "I'll do everything I can."

CHAPTER 17

As soon as he could, Beryl went to Vilna to find out about our money. I was waiting on the road when he got back, wanting to be the first to know.

Then I raced home. "Ma!" I exclaimed. "We're going to America!"

Ma clapped her hands over her heart. Tears welled in her eyes. She sat down—as if the news was too much for her. "Oh! What a miracle, America!" She patted her heart to calm it down. "Oh my goodness! I'll send for Rifka right away!" Her face lit up as I'd never seen before.

"Rifka?" I asked.

"Who's Rifka?" asked Benyomin.

"Oh, my goodness." Ma looked suddenly sad. "You don't know, do you?" She turned to me and then to Benyomin and said quietly, "Rifka is your sister."

Our sister? My mouth dropped open.

"We have *another* sister?" asked Benyomin.

Ma nodded. "You don't remember her, do you?" But she said it more to herself than to us.

"Well I remember her!" Kvola burst out. "I remember everything. *They* were both too little. But I'll never forget when Grandfather took Rifka away in his wagon. I was so mad. I tried to kick him." She gave a strong kick at the air. "I started to run after the wagon, but you held me back."

Ma nodded. "It took all my strength." She looked sadly from me to Benyomin. "You don't remember Rifka at all?"

"It's no wonder!" Now Hannah spoke up. "You never even let us *mention* her. I was afraid she was dead. You always hushed us. *Always.*" Hannah, who never raised her voice, had all this spilling out of her. "Why, Ma? Why was it so terrible to even say her name?"

Ma closed her eyes for a second. Then quietly looking down at her hands, she spoke: "It was too hard. You can't imagine. It hurt too much." She shook her head, and pressed some tears away with the corner of her apron. "I was beginning to think I'd never get her back." She turned to me and Benyomin. "When you were very little, your grandparents—Pa's parents—took Rifka to make it easier on me until Pa sent for us." Ma sighed. "I never thought it would take this long. Never." She got a faraway look, as if watching from a long time ago. "I wonder how big she is now." Her voice grew soft and melting. "She was such a little girl back then."

Rifka, I thought to myself. Rifka. So that's what Ma had meant by "one child poorer."

I have another sister, I told myself trying to make it real. Rifka. Another sister. I wonder what she's like.

Suddenly Ma jumped up and clapped her hands to her cheeks. "The money!" she exclaimed. "Heaven forbid anything should happen to it now. We're so close. We must get boat tickets right away! *Ai, yai, yai.*" She rocked her head in her hands. "Boat tickets! How will we get them? Someone must buy them for us. But who? Who can we trust not to run off with our money? Or, heaven forbid, send us to the wrong place? I must speak with Beryl right away."

She hurried out. I ran after her, anxious to hear everything.

"Calm down," Beryl told Ma, as soon as she blurted out her fears. "I know of some people in Vilna. They won't steal your money," he promised. "They'll buy your tickets and arrange everything. Don't worry."

Of course Ma worried. We all did. Even though we trusted Beryl, how could we be sure about these other people? But finally Ma told Beryl, yes, he should give them our money. Then she sent a message to Grandfather telling him to bring Rifka. There was a lot for Ma to worry about getting everything ready. All new problems. Ma called them *zisseh tsuris.* Sweet problems.

Soon it seemed everyone in the *shtetl* had heard we were going to America. People started coming to say good-bye and wish us a safe journey. I'd often see Ma and Hannah and Kvola hugging neighbors and friends, all crying together.

"Why are you crying?" I asked Hannah one time.

"It's hard to say good-bye," she told me.

But it wasn't hard for me. We were going to America! I wasn't crying. I could hardly wait. I went to the shoemaker to tell him I'd be wearing his boots to America.

"So, *my* boots will touch American soil," he said wistfully. "I'm glad they still fit you."

I didn't tell him that, by now, they were so tight my toes curled under and that Ma kept scolding me to stop wearing them.

I planned to arrive in America in my leather boots no matter what—not in some dead soldier's shoes, like Benyomin's. He'd found them after the *pogrom*. They were so big they kept flopping off his feet. That's not how I wanted to set foot in America. No thank you!

The days sped on. Even though we'd be leaving soon, Ma said Benyomin and I still had to go to *heder.* One day I stumbled over the words of a prayer I should have known easily. The teacher grabbed his stick and held it over my head. "Pay attention!" he warned. I shrank away from the stick. "Fivel! Listen to me! Soon you'll be learning a whole new language and even a new alphabet. Don't forget what you already know." He shook the stick over my head. I nodded vigorously that I wouldn't. *"And,"* he went on, bringing the stick even closer, "don't ever forget who you are!" He looked at me sternly and I kept nodding. "Do you hear me, Fivel?"

"Yes," I said. "Don't forget who I am." But to myself, I thought, Is he *meshuggeneh*? How can I ever forget who I am? It made no sense. And it wouldn't for a long time.

Meanwhile, it seemed like forever since the package had arrived. Sometimes I'd trace my finger around Pa's face in the photograph, look into his eyes, and whisper, "We're coming, Pa. We're coming."

Finally one morning, Ma told us, "We'll be leaving tomorrow."

After *heder,* Benyomin and I ran around playing with the other boys. It seemed just like any other day. But every so often, a thought came flying in: *I'm leaving tomorrow.* And I'd feel strangely loose and bouncy inside. *Leaving,* I'd remind myself. *For America.*

CHAPTER 18

That afternoon, Ma called us together. "We're going to Beryl's. It's time to say good-bye."

Beryl's face lit up when we came through his door. "Well, look who's here. The whole family! What's the occasion?" As if he didn't know . . .

Ma tried to smile. "We came to say good-bye."

"Just think! You're going to America! I'm so happy for you." He gave a big smile. But his eyes looked sad.

Ma ran her hand along the big wooden counter. "We can't thank you enough, Beryl. Without you . . ." Her lip quivered. She tried again. "Without you . . ." But she shook her head, and couldn't say more. "Thank you," she finally squeezed out.

"Oh, please!" Beryl touched her arm. "There's nothing to thank." Ma tried to say something else, but her face crumpled like an empty flour sack. Tears rolled down her cheeks. She bit her lower lip, unable to go on.

Hannah, always so quiet, was the one who spoke up. "You've been so good to us, Beryl. You've helped us more than we can ever say." Her eyes brimmed with tears. "We can never thank you enough. Never." It came in a rush, as if from a sudden, urgent place inside.

I wanted to say something, too. But I didn't know what.

Benyomin spoke up, "Thank you for all the food." His voice shook. "You kept us alive."

Kvola, who usually had so much to say, was sobbing so hard she couldn't speak. Even *I* was getting teary. And I still hadn't said a word.

"Stop it already." Beryl rubbed his eyes and blinked hard. "You'd all better get out of here before we have a flood." He hugged each of us. "Now take good care of each other. And have a safe journey."

"Thank you, Beryl. Good-bye." Ma opened the door and rushed out. Hannah, Kvola, and Benyomin followed.

But I still wanted to tell him something. I just wasn't sure what. I looked up, trying to memorize his face and fix it deep inside me. His kind eyes. His warm, open smile.

He wrapped his big arms around me. "Well, my Fivel, soon you'll get to see your *real* pa." And the way he said it poked a place inside me I hadn't known was there.

He rocked me back and forth, back and forth. "And before you know it . . ." His voice caught in his throat and became a scratchy whisper. "Before you know it, you'll . . ." He gave a sigh. Then, all husky and quiet, "Try to remember me, Fivel." He gave a squeeze and dropped his arms.

Try to remember him? What a strange thing to say. "Of course I'll remember you." How could I ever forget Beryl?

"Fivel, my sweet boy." Beryl smoothed my hair. "You're starting a new life. I only wish I could see you grow up." His face was wet with tears.

Me? Grow up? What a thought. I couldn't really imagine it. It was too far off. But, even so, a part of me must have always figured on Beryl being there. Now a sudden, breathless feeling swept through me. He wouldn't be. I'd been so afraid he'd leave us. And now we were leaving him.

To America. It had always been impossibly far away. But soon we'd be there. Maybe someday, just like that, I'd suddenly find myself all grown up. My head whirled at the thought. Well, I sure hoped Ma would be right about me.

"Ma always tells me I should grow up to be like you—with a big heart," I said. Although saying it aloud, it seemed more impossible than anything.

Beryl rubbed his eyes with the heel of his hand. "Does she really?" He looked pleased and sad at the same time.

"Yes." I nodded. "I doubt that I can, but I'll try."

"You're growing up just fine," he said. I wasn't so sure about that. But I hoped he was right. He gently kissed the top of my head. "So you'll think of me sometimes?"

"All the time," I promised, believing with all my heart

that I would. I drank in his warm, comforting smell. Flour and yeast and fresh baked bread.

"I'll think of you, too, my Fivel." He handed me some rolls. "Have a safe journey."

"Thank you." I stuffed them into my pocket. "I wish I had something to give *you*." This was my last chance and, still, I had nothing.

Beryl gazed at me with a soft, sad smile. "You should only know how much you've given me, Fivel." He held his hand over his heart. "You should only know." I didn't know exactly what he meant by that, but somehow, I could feel it when I looked in his eyes.

I didn't know what to say. I tore out of there, startled by the tears flying off my face.

CHAPTER 19

The next morning, Ma wrapped our blankets around our Sabbath candlesticks and wooden bowls and spoons. She put them into a sack. Then she carefully wrapped Pa's picture and slid it in. Even with these few things packed, our house was already looking empty and deserted.

Ma said we'd have to leave everything else—the table and chairs, the wood plates and cooking pots. Benyomin and I begged to take our wheel. But Ma said there was no room. Of course, Hannah took her few needles and thread. And Kvola insisted on taking a small copper cup that she and Ma used for grinding. She said she *must* have it. I knew what she meant. That's how I felt about my boots, which, of course, I was wearing.

Now all we could do was wait for Grandfather—Pa's pa to come bring Rifka in his wagon and take us all to Vilna. Ma said he lived more than a two days' walk from us. That's why we'd never visited him. She also said maybe it was for the best. It would've been too hard to see Rifka and not bring her home.

Now we stood outside, watching the road for Grandfather's horse and wagon. Ma said he and Grandmother had an apple orchard. So I knew they must be rich. That's why they could afford to take Rifka. I hopped from one foot to the other—impatient to see her.

Ma gave my hand a gentle squeeze. She took her eyes off the road a second and looked down at me. "Rifka will be surprised at how big you are." But I wondered if Rifka would even remember me.

Suddenly a horse-drawn wagon came into view over the far hill. "There's Rifka!" Ma's cheeks grew pink with excitement.

I could barely see her. But I saw Grandfather, sitting high on the seat, straight and tall holding the reins. It was still too far for me to see his face. He looked like most other Jewish men in our *shtetl* with his round, black hat and long beard. As the wagon drew closer, I could see that Rifka looked older than Benyomin. Too bad. She was probably too old to play with us.

"Look at that wagon!" Benyomin exclaimed. It was as big as Beryl's. "I bet their house is big, too!"

"With lots of food," I said quietly—out of Ma's earshot. "Lucky Rifka."

But Ma heard. She took her eyes off the wagon just long enough to give me a hard, stern look. "Remember that rich man who wanted to take you?" That's all she had to say. But she went on anyway. "You think Rifka wanted to leave home?" Her voice cracked but then turned sharp. "She had no choice. We knew it wasn't forever—though, believe me, it seemed like that. Would you have wanted to switch places with her?"

"No." I shook my head vigorously. I watched the wagon draw closer. Rifka did look well fed. I wouldn't have minded *that* part of it. But I didn't say so.

As soon as the wagon stopped, Ma rushed over with arms outstretched. "Rifka!"

Grandfather helped Rifka down. Before she'd set both feet on the ground, she was in Ma's arms.

"Rifkala, oh my Rifkala." Tears streamed down Ma's cheeks. "You're such a big girl! Let me look at you." She held her at arm's length for a moment and then pulled her back close—sobbing. "Oh, my Rifkala."

I stood by watching with wonder. That's my sister, I told myself, still getting used to the idea. Her wool sweater looked nicer than any Ma or Kvola or Hannah ever had. And her cheeks were plump and healthy looking. But she'd been away from Ma for such a long time—almost my whole life. No, I didn't envy her.

We all stood watching, feeling a little shy—except for Kvola, who rushed right up. "Rifka, look at you. You're so big!" she exclaimed. "Where's my little sister?" She gave her a nudge. "Is that really you? No!"

Rifka let out a delighted giggle. "It's me all right. But is this *you,* Kvola?" She stood tall measuring herself to Kvola. They were almost eye to eye. "I'm catching up to you." She giggled again in that playful, teasing way.

"You'd better watch out!" Already I was beginning to like her.

My grandfather looked handsome in his black sheep's wool hat and his long black *kaputah,* which came down almost to his ankles. He hugged each of us. "Fivel, you're so big." He beamed at me. Oh, that made me feel good. That's my pa's pa I told myself proudly. Soon, I'll meet my pa.

Now Grandfather helped Ma into the front seat while the rest of us climbed into the back of the wagon. There was a load of apples back there. They looked good and juicy.

Grandfather handed one to each of us. "Eat," he said. "Eat as many as you want. It's what's left from last season."

I didn't need any encouragement. I crunched into my apple and hoped the trip to Vilna would last a good, long time. The sweetness filled my mouth. All of us took big thirsty bites—even Ma. All except Rifka. She took small polite bites as if this was nothing new for her. I guess it wasn't. But for us, the only apples we ever ate were the ones we found rotting on the ground in someone's orchard or the few good ones we managed to swipe off the trees. No one just handed us apples and said, "Eat."

Kvola sat right close to Rifka. They were already chattering and laughing as if they'd always been together. Like me and Benyomin I thought—always together. Then I remembered that awful emptiness when we'd thought he was dead. An emptiness nothing could fill. Was it like that for Kvola when they took Rifka away? And for Ma, too, and probably Hannah? Now with Kvola and Rifka chattering, Hannah seemed even quieter and more to herself.

She gazed out along the road at the passing hills, as if tugged by her own thoughts. She caught me watching. "Take a good look, Fivel," she whispered. "You'll never see this again."

Sometimes with Hannah, it seemed that she saw more than the rest of us. She spent more time thinking instead of talking. I tried to see it her way now. I gazed out, but all I saw were hills and mountains and our *shtetl*. Not whatever Hannah saw. All I could think was, we're heading for America. A whole new life. With *Pa*. No more problems.

No war, hunger, Cossacks, or *pogroms*. What other troubles could there be? None that I knew of, that was for sure.

My grandfather snapped the reins. We clopped along the dirt road—leaving the *shtetl* farther and farther behind. I glanced back again.

There was Beryl outside feeding his chickens—already looking small and faraway.

I jumped up. "Beryl!" I shouted and waved hard as I could.

Hannah pulled me down. "Careful! You'll fall out," she warned.

"Anyway, he can't hear you," said Kvola.

But I kept waving. "Beryl!" I called with all my heart. "Beryl!" Just as we reached the top of the hill, Beryl looked up. I know he saw me. He gave a long full sweep of his arm. The wagon dipped down the other side of the hill, swallowing my view.

Now all I could see was the road. No Beryl. No *shtetl.* No use looking back. We were on our way to a new life. I turned forward and settled in for the ride. I wanted to see exactly where I was going and not miss a thing.

CHAPTER 20

We traveled that same road, on and on, past great sweeps of mountains, green stretches of hills, and flat open fields scattered with small farms. I'd already eaten plenty of apples. And by now, my poor bottom was sore from so much sitting and jostling. I was itching to get out and stretch.

Finally Grandfather called back to us, "We're coming into Vilna. Get ready."

Vilna!

As we drew into the bustling city, every street was an eyeful—all the people in their fine clothes, the horse-drawn carriages, the tall buildings. Vilna was so much bigger than our *shtetl.* How would Grandfather ever find the person Beryl had given our money to?

But I barely had time to worry. Before long, Grandfather announced, "Here's the train station."

We clambered out of the wagon. Oh, did it feel good to stretch my legs! Grandfather looked around the station and quickly strode over to a lady wearing a white cap with a bright red cross on it. We all hurried behind him, with Ma clutching our sack of belongings.

"Do you have tickets for the Myzels?" he asked the lady. "They're traveling to America." My grandfather spoke to her for a while. Finally she handed certain papers to Ma explaining that they were for our passage to America. It made my heart leap to see them in Ma's hand. I stood on tiptoe to take a better look.

Strange loops, lines, and curves filled the page—so different from any letters I'd ever learned in *heder.* This must be the new alphabet my teacher had told me about. Would I ever be able to read such peculiar marks? Would they ever look as familiar as Hebrew?

Now the lady smiled down at me. "I'm sure you know that you must always stay with your family."

"Yes." I nodded, burrowing close to Ma. Of course I knew that.

"The train will be here soon," she told us. "If you need any help along the way, find someone wearing a white cap like mine with this red cross on it. We're from the Red Cross. And we're here to help you."

The Red Cross. They must be the people Beryl had told Ma about. This lady did seem like someone we could trust.

My grandfather waited on the platform with us, his arm around Rifka's shoulder—holding her close. His face, which had looked so bright this morning, was now drawn and solemn.

Suddenly a great thundering filled my ears. The floor shuddered under my feet. "Here comes the train,"

Grandfather shouted over the rumbling. It rushed toward us like a huge metal beast, snorting louder than any horses I'd ever heard. My heart pounded almost as loudly. The train hissed to a stop. The doors rolled open. People started piling in.

Grandfather held Rifka in a tight hug. "Oh my Rifkala." He squeezed his eyes shut.

"Good-bye, *Zayde,*" Rifka choked out.

"Now don't cry," said Grandfather. But his lips were trembling and his eyes watered. "Send my love to your pa."

Rifka nodded. "I will, *Zayde.*" She bit her lower lip and sniffed hard.

The train was filling up. I was afraid it would leave without us. I started to run toward it.

"Wait!" yelled Ma. "Don't go running off like that!" She grabbed hold of my hand so tight my knuckles crunched together. "Hang onto each other." She gave me a stern look and then shot that same look at Benyomin and my sisters. "Stay together. If any of you gets lost, I'll never find you."

Seeing the great mass of people all around us, I realized Ma was right. Quickly, I grabbed Benyomin's hand. Kvola grabbed Rifka's. Hannah was on Rifka's other side but stood there for a moment, too shy to take her hand. Instead, Kvola reached over and grabbed Hannah's hand.

Meanwhile, I was all jumpy, itching to get on the train.

Ma looked up at Grandfather. "Thank you for all your help." Then she told us, "Say good-bye to your grandfather." So we all did. But Rifka was the only one who looked truly sad.

"Please, Ma," I urged. "The train!"

Finally Ma nodded. And we all rushed on—still holding hands.

By now, there was no place to sit. Polish soldiers had already taken all the seats. And the aisles were so packed with people standing there wasn't even room for me to sit on the floor. A wrinkled old woman barely kept her balance, as the doors closed and the train lurched forward.

It was hot and smelly in there. Some soldiers were eating salt pork and dark bread. They scraped the white layer of salt off the meat and cut thick, fatty slices for themselves. Even though Jews aren't supposed to eat pork, my mouth watered. If one of the soldiers offers me a slice, I thought, I don't know if I'll be able to refuse. But no one offered. I dug into my pocket and felt the three rolls from Beryl. I fingered one for a while and brought it up to my lips. Ma looked down at me, surprised.

"It's from Beryl," I explained.

"Nu?" She raised an eyebrow. "You think we're not hungry, too?"

Stinging with shame, I quickly broke it into pieces. Just yesterday I'd told Beryl I wanted to be like him—

with a big heart. And already I'd almost eaten the whole roll by myself—not even thinking. I counted the pieces. Not five anymore. Six. One for Rifka who'd always had plenty to eat.

"Thank you, Fivel!" She looked as grateful as any of us. I suppose even people who are well fed can still be hungry, I told myself. But I wasn't totally convinced.

I watched Rifka, in her nice sweater, taking small, careful bites, making it last just like the rest of us. Beryl would be glad to see her eating his roll. I tried to be glad, too.

Every now and then, Ma looked at Rifka in a strange way. "Oh, Rifkala," she'd say and smooth Rifka's cheek with her fingertips, as if trying to find the face of the little girl who'd left years ago. She'd pat Rifka's hand and say, "You're my Rifkala," with such love that I wished she'd say something like that to me.

The train sped on and on. I stood squashed between Ma and Benyomin, badly wanting to see out the window. But there were too many people blocking the view. I could barely breathe. Hannah, Rifka, and Kvola were squeezed next to us, worn and tired. The wrinkled old woman looked worse than any of us. She leaned against Ma. I wondered if her feet would hold her up much longer. Ma must've been wondering the same thing.

She stared at a nearby soldier, her lips pressed tightly together, until finally he got up and gave the old woman his seat. I watched as she settled herself down. Her shoulders slumped and her cheeks puffed with a grateful sigh. My whole body ached to sit.

Finally, the train stopped.

"Hurry, Ma!" I tugged her arm, pushing toward the door.

"No." She shook her head. "We don't get off until Warsaw."

"How far is that?"

Ma shrugged. "Go to sleep. It's late."

The doors closed and the train lurched forward, bumping us into each other. Leaning against Ma, I nodded off to sleep. But at every stop, I woke up. "Is this it?"

"Not yet. Go back to sleep." And somehow I'd fall back to sleep standing up. We stood all through the night jostling back and forth. Early the next morning, the train slowed down and a loud, clear voice called out, "Warsaw!" The train came to a jerky stop and the doors rolled open. I pushed my way toward them.

"Fivel!" Ma called sternly. "Hold my hand!" She crushed my hand in hers. "Hang on to each other!" she ordered all of us. "If you get lost, I'll never find you."

CHAPTER 21

Benyomin and I quickly grabbed hands. Kvola grabbed Rifka's hand. Then Hannah reached over and grabbed Kvola's other hand. I was so afraid the train would leave and we'd still be on it—grabbing hands.

"Please, Ma!" I begged. As soon as she nodded, we all rushed onto the platform. The station was even bigger than Vilna's. What a place! People were hurrying in every direction.

"Where do we go?" I asked Ma.

"I'm not sure yet." Her forehead creased.

I jumped up and down to see over people's heads.

"Look!" I pointed to the far end of the station. "There's a Red Cross lady." Relief washed over Ma's face—which made me proud.

We rushed straight there. A whole group of people, all with sacks like Ma's, were already gathered around. The lady checked our papers and wrote something down. Then she led the whole group out of the station.

I squinted in the bright sunlight. Tall buildings towered like giants. They must have eight or even nine floors. What a huge city Warsaw was! Horse-drawn trolley cars rolled on skinny metal tracks. Big horses trotted along the streets pulling beautiful carriages. There were even shiny black automobiles running without any horses. It gave me a rich feeling just looking at all this.

The Red Cross lady brought us to a tall building. She said this is where we'd stay until the boat arrived. She took us to a large room with many people like us—all with sacks of belongings, all waiting for the boat to America. Ma laid our blankets on some rusty metal beds with thin mattresses. This is where we'd sleep.

Right away, I noticed something amazing. There were glass bulbs that lit up when a worker lifted a small knob.

"How does it do that?" I asked him.

"Electricity," he said, as if that explained it. I wondered if there was electricity in America and if Pa had some.

Equally amazing was an indoor toilet down the hall. "How does the water get here? Where does it come from?" I asked—fascinated by the rush of water that spurted into the bowl.

"Pipes and plumbing," the worker said. But again, that didn't really explain anything to me. This was a whole new world.

At first it seemed such a treat to have an indoor toilet. But since there was only one, whenever we needed to use it, we had to wait in line. There were also long lines to get our meals, which were mostly cooked cabbage and potatoes.

Kvola and Rifka seemed to find endless things to talk and laugh about. Hannah mainly listened. Ma said she was getting to know Rifka in her own way. But what about me, I wondered. Rifka's *my* sister, too.

Day by day, the room got stuffier and smellier. I'd take out Pa's picture and tell him, "We're coming, Pa. We're coming." But I was beginning to wonder *when*.

Finally one morning, there was an announcement: "The ship has arrived in Rotterdam! Get ready for the train."

The train? Not another one! But Ma was already folding our blankets and stuffing them into the sack. Everyone was packing as fast as possible. It would be a mad rush for the train station. I dashed for the door. "I'll get us some seats," I called, determined I'd *sit* this time.

"No! Stay with me!" Ma insisted. "Hang onto each other. If you get lost—"

Kvola cut in, "We know, Ma." And she finished in a singsong voice, "If we get lost, you'll never find us." She looked at Rifka and they both burst into giggles.

"That's right," said Ma sternly. "Now do it."

I quickly took hold of Ma's and Benyomin's hands. Kvola took Rifka's. And this time, Hannah took Rifka's other hand. Rifka looked pleased to be in between her two sisters. I guess Ma was right about Hannah.

We quickly headed for the train. It was just as crowded and smelly as the last one. And again, no luck with seats. I was already tired of trains. And this ride was even longer than the other one. By the time we reached Rotterdam, I never wanted to see another train.

But the ship, well, that was a different story! When we arrived at the pier, my mouth dropped wide open. That ship towered above us like a mountain. Masses of people stood gazing at it. I tilted my head way back. It filled the whole dock and half the sky. I felt awfully small.

"Hang on to each other." Ma's voice was tense. But this time, she didn't need to remind me. I gripped her hand and Benyomin's, good and tight, as we headed up the gangplank.

Ma glanced behind to check our sisters. "Hannah! Rifka!" Panic rose in her voice. "Where's Kvola?" Benyomin and I turned to see. Hannah and Rifka were right behind us holding hands. But not Kvola.

Hannah looked around. "Where can she be?"

Ma scanned the crowd. "How could she disappear?"

"I'm—I'm sorry," Rifka whimpered, giving Ma a pleading look. "She only let go for a minute. She said she'd catch up." Ma didn't waste time scolding. She stretched her neck high, searching the crowd.

The ship blasted a loud warning. Then came the call, "All aboard!"

The crowd pressed forward carrying us with it.

"I must find her." Ma's voice rose sharp and urgent. She pushed us over to the side. "Stay right here. Don't move! Take this—" She shoved the sack at Hannah.

Hannah clutched it to her chest. "But what if . . ." The rest of her thought loomed unspoken.

Rifka looked sick with fear, and guilt, too, I thought. She was the one who'd let go. Ma must be furious with her.

Poor Rifka. I took her hand and patted it. "Everything will be all right." I gave a squeeze. But in my head, Ma's words echoed. *If any of you gets lost, I'll never find you.*

CHAPTER 22

The boat blasted another warning. "All aboard!"

Benyomin and I looked at each other but didn't say a word.

I stood on tiptoe, searching the crowd for Ma. But all I saw were strangers—all with bundles, all heading onto the boat for America.

I tried to push away the questions. But they came anyway. *What if Ma doesn't find her? What then? What if the boat is about to leave and Ma's not here?* No. I mustn't think that way. Ma would say, Bite your tongue.

Benyomin tugged my sleeve. "Look! Here comes Ma!" And there she was, plowing her way back through the crowd. And there, thank goodness, was Kvola, right behind her, her face flushed. A wave of relief swept through me all the way down to my toes.

"Kvola!" Hannah cried. "We were so worried!"

"What happened? Where were you?" Rifka grabbed her hand so hard Kvola winced.

"I'm sorry." Kvola cast her eyes down. "I only just stopped to talk for a minute."

"To a stranger!" Ma spat out the words. "Imagine!"

Kvola blushed a deep red. "I didn't know you'd gone so far ahead." From the look of her flushed cheeks, I guessed that the stranger must have been a handsome one. Despite all she'd put us through, I couldn't help noticing how pretty and grown-up she looked. That's our Kvola, I thought.

"Let's go!" I grabbed Ma's hand and pulled. She looked weary as we headed up the gangplank. But not me. I was bouncing. We were on our way to America! "Don't forget," I sang out. "Hang onto each other!" I shot a grin at Rifka.

She shot one back at me and leaned down close to my ear. "*Oy!* Was I scared!"

I nodded back at her. "Me, too! Worse than anything."

"Not worse than me!" She giggled. And right then I started to feel she was my real sister.

"This way!" two men in uniform barked at us. "This way down to steerage!" They herded all of us along. I badly wanted to take a look around the ship. But I only got a quick glimpse before they'd hustled us down some stairs. It was so dark I could barely see the steps. Down, down, flight after flight, it got darker and smellier.

Finally we came to a dim room way in the belly of the ship. By now, our eyes were used to the faint light. But our noses weren't used to the smell. The air was so thick it could've been shoveled in.

Kvola made a face. "It's worse than an outhouse." She covered her nose.

"Uh!" "It is!" *"Feh!"* We all agreed and covered our noses.

But Ma wasn't interested in our complaints. "You'll get used to it," she said. And while all of us were covering our noses, she claimed some of the lower metal bunk beds and laid out our blankets. People who weren't so quick ended up cramped in the upper bunks. We felt lucky to have the floor right by our beds.

The mattresses were thin and tattered. But we made ourselves as comfortable as possible. I took a few careful breaths. Uh! It smelled like rotten food, stinking bodies, and stale air. *Feh!*

That night, I took another roll from my pocket and broke it into pieces. By now it was easy to make six instead of five.

I handed them out and held mine to my nose, trying to smell the sweetness of Beryl's bakery. But I barely smelled anything beyond the heavy air of steerage. I closed my eyes. Beryl's kind face smiled at me. I patted the last roll in my pocket and whispered, "Thank you" and slowly ate my share.

I took out Pa's picture. "We're on our way," I told him. "Soon, Pa. Soon."

CHAPTER 23

It didn't take us long to get tired of that ship. Day after day we got the same thing to eat—cooked cabbage and potatoes and watered-down soup. There wasn't much of anything to see or do. But, unfortunately, there was plenty to smell. More by the day. Most of the food that people had brought along was rotting by now. On top of that, all the unwashed bodies, cooked cabbage, people getting seasick, and who knows what else, made a powerful smell.

But one day, I heard some faint music. So beautiful! It sounded like heaven.

"Benyomin, where's that music coming from?" I looked around, although I knew it wasn't from anywhere nearby.

"Upstairs." He lifted his eyes.

I nodded. "Maybe the rich people are having a dance." I pictured them in fancy clothes dancing to this beautiful music. I tried to imagine what *they* must be smelling up there—all kinds of delicious foods, no doubt. Naturally, I didn't only imagine how good their food must smell. I also began to imagine how good it must taste.

"I'm getting awfully tired of cabbage and potatoes," I said quietly—even though we were far out of Ma's earshot. "And I'm sick of that watery soup they give us." I wrinkled my nose.

"Me, too," Benyomin agreed.

"I wonder what the rich people are eating." I eyed the big, heavy door to the stairs.

Who knows what we'd find upstairs. Maybe a little bit of something delicious. Maybe we'd even sneak some back in our pockets.

I glanced over at Ma. She was busy talking with some other women. She wouldn't notice if we were gone for a little while. Neither would our sisters. They were chatting away with some other girls. Of course, Hannah was mostly listening. But her back was to us.

Benyomin looked at me. I looked back at him. "I'll go if you do," I whispered, wondering if he'd dare.

He looked over at Ma. She was still talking. To my surprise, Benyomin nodded. "All right. But just a quick look."

"We'll be back before anyone notices," I agreed.

We sneaked over to the heavy door, yanked it open together, and slipped through.

The door shut solidly behind us. We were in total darkness.

I felt around with my foot and found the steps. Carefully, carefully, I started climbing. With each step, the music grew louder and the air grew fresher. My heart galloped and my mouth watered as we hurried up flight after flight.

Finally, we came to a door. Without thinking twice, I pushed it open. Suddenly we were in glaring daylight, so bright I couldn't see at first. But once I got used to it, what a world it was!

Endless ocean in all directions. More water than I'd ever imagined. Now I could see for myself that Kvola had been right. This ocean was way too big for any bridge to stretch across it.

We looked over the railing. It was awfully dark down there. And deep! I held on tight. Just looking at all that water made me breathless. If someone fell in, by mistake, that would be the end of him for sure. But we were safe with this strong, sturdy railing. I looked around. No one else was out here. Everyone must be at the dance.

I took a big breath of fresh air. What a treat! Of course we had other treats in mind, too.

"Come on," I urged. "Let's see what we can find."

"Yeah, but which way do we go?" asked Benyomin.

We listened carefully and started down a hallway. The music grew louder. At the far end, there were large double doors. I pushed one open just a crack and peeked in.

We'd found it all right. There were people in fancy clothes and tables covered with white tablecloths and, oh, such delicious-looking food! So many kinds of cookies and luscious creamy sweets—just waiting to be plucked off those big platters. My mouth watered.

All we needed to do was scoot in and slip over to that table. I licked my lips. Even a tiny nibble would be worth the risk. I opened the door a crack more and took one careful step forward.

"Stop right there!" growled a deep voice behind me.

CHAPTER 24

Two big sailors loomed over us.

"Filthy ragamuffins!" snarled one in Russian. "You don't belong here."

"Little thieves!" growled the other. "What did you steal?"

My heart knocked against my ribs. Benyomin looked at me in terror. We both knew enough Russian to clearly understand the sailors. But I also knew that Benyomin wouldn't say a word.

I opened my mouth. "We . . . we . . ." My throat was all tight. "We—we were just looking." It came out small and squeaky.

"Sure, sure," the first one sneered.

Then before we knew what was happening, they'd grabbed us by the seats of our pants and the backs of our collars and hauled us down the long hall and onto the deck.

"This is what we do with little thieves," snarled the one holding me. He swung me out over the railing. My stomach reeled to my throat.

"Dirty little thief!" He shook me over the water. "You won't ever steal anything again." He snorted a big nasty laugh.

My mouth went dry as paper. *Yell for help,* I urged myself. *Yell!* But my throat was squeezed shut.

Benyomin whimpered, dangling over the water, too.

"Heave!" they shouted.

The whole big ocean came lurching at us—tilting, reeling, upside-down.

"Heave!" They swung us farther.

Any second they'd drop us. Into that deep, dark water. No one would even see. *Poor Ma. She'd never know what happened to us. Poor Ma. After all she's been through.* And somehow, that brought my voice back. LOUD.

"Help!" I screamed with all my guts. "HELP!"

"Shut up, you little idiot!" the sailor holding me shouted. Still, I kept screaming, "HELP! HELP!"

"Troublemaker!" he snarled. "Shut up!" He yanked me back inside the railing and set me down hard on my feet. He leaned into my face so close I could see big dark pores on his nose. "Get outta here!" He aimed a kick at me.

My legs wobbled. I gripped the railing to keep from falling. My head whirled.

Benyomin was still hanging over the water, pale as death.

"Please don't drop him," I begged. *"Please."*

The sailor holding Benyomin gave his buddy an evil smile. "Should I?"

"Sure," sneered the other. "The little thief deserves it."

"Here goes." He swung him way out.

"NO!" I cried. "HELP!" I turned to see if help was coming.

"SHUT UP!" The sailor shot me an angry look, but I kept screaming. My heart pounded in my throat. "Help!" I yelled again. I thought I heard footsteps. "HELP!" I screamed, fearing that whoever was coming would get here too late.

"Hey, someone's coming," called his buddy.

"Who cares?" he sneered. But to my utter relief, he swung Benyomin back inside the railing and set him down on the deck. Hard.

Benyomin's legs wobbled. I grabbed his arm and pulled him straight for those stairs. Fast.

"Scram!" they shouted as we flew down. "And don't come back!" They snorted ugly laughs like it was some big joke.

My heart galloped faster than my feet. My insides shook. What if they'd dropped us? It made my stomach reel. All that water. So deep. The ship would've kept going. We'd be left. Two little specks in that big dark ocean.

I couldn't stop these terrible thoughts. We'd drown. Ma would never know. Poor Ma!

By the time we pushed through the heavy door, back into steerage, tears were streaming down my face.

"Don't tell Ma!" I wailed in big gasps.

"She'd kill us." Benyomin sobbed.

Ma spotted us and rushed over. "Where were you? I was worried sick."

We flung ourselves into her arms. "Ma!" I cried. "Oh, Ma!" My whole body was trembling.

"What's the matter?" She held us to her. "What happened?"

She didn't have to ask twice. In heaving sobs, I blurted out, "They—almost—drowned us!"

"Who?" Ma urged. "Who would do such a thing?"

"The sailors," Benyomin wailed, ". . . over the railing!"

"No!" Ma gasped in horror.

"Yes," I burrowed closer.

"What were you doing up there?"

"Nothing." I cradled into her arms. "Just looking for the music. We didn't take any food." I wiped my nose on my sleeve. "They said we did. But we didn't."

"Thank goodness you're safe!" Ma held us more tightly. "Those rotten sailors!"

I nodded, "But I screamed real loud and they put us down."

"Thankfully!" Ma squeezed us.

"But we almost drowned," I said again—to keep her arms around me as long as I could. "We were almost dead."

She stroked the tears off my cheeks. "It's all right now. Don't worry." She didn't even yell at us for going off. She rocked us both in her arms and said, "It's all right" over and over.

CHAPTER 25

Land! That's what Benyomin and I heard one day. Land in sight! Word spread quickly around steerage. The news lifted everyone's spirits. We'd been on the boat for over two smelly weeks. It seemed like years. Soon we'd be in America!

We'd heard rumors that before they let us in, we'd first stay on a place called Ellis Island in New York harbor where they'd make sure we were healthy. If we weren't, they'd send us back on the next boat. Ma was terribly worried. But Kvola said she didn't believe they could possibly do that since we'd paid all that money from Pa to get here.

Naturally, we hoped Kvola was right. Being down in steerage hadn't done us any good. Even Rifka didn't have that well-fed, rosy look anymore. By now, her clothes were almost as shabby as ours. But no one else down here looked any better. They wouldn't send us all back. Would they?

By evening, as we drew closer to shore, everyone in steerage was allowed to come up on deck. I hadn't gone near those stairs since that scary day.

Now, as we climbed flight after flight, Ma held our sack under one arm and gripped my hand with the other. "Stay right with me. Don't go wandering off." She gave my hand a hard squeeze. But she didn't have to. I knew!

At last we reached open air. I tilted my head back, held my mouth wide open, and drew in a big fresh breath. Ma drew in a deep breath, too. "Oh! A *mechaieh!*" A great pleasure! I enjoyed her delight. But even with all this fresh air, that foul smell of steerage hung on our clothes.

The sun had already set so it wasn't glaring bright like last time. Fortunately there was still some light. I wanted to see *everything*. As we slowly entered New York harbor, we gaped at the tall buildings—much taller than any we'd seen even in Warsaw. How could they stand so high up and not fall down? I couldn't imagine.

Suddenly people all around us were pointing at the biggest lady I'd ever seen.

"Look at her, Benyomin!" I pointed, too.

"Ooh! Who is she?" he exclaimed. The lady was holding a book in one hand and a torch in the other. She was all lit up.

"It's a statue," said Ma.

"What is she doing here?" I asked.

One man tugged my sleeve. All excited, he pointed and tried to explain. But he spoke a language I'd never heard before.

"Do you speak Yiddish?" I asked. "Or Polish?" He just

shrugged. "Russian?" I tried. But he shook his head. People were talking about that lady in all different languages. Finally, I heard a woman speaking Yiddish. I tapped her arm. "Who is that beautiful, shining lady?"

"That's the Statue of Liberty," she said in a hushed voice as if she were in a synagogue. "She's here for all the immigrants—people like us—who are starting a new life in America." Her eyes watered. "Can you imagine? She's here to welcome us." Tears rolled down her cheeks.

Such a big beautiful statue for people like us? Already, I liked America. If they had a statue like this for someone like me, it must be a good place to live.

I took the last roll out of my pocket. It was old and hard by now. But I broke it into six pieces. Everyone in my family took one. We ate slowly—savoring what only we could taste in these stale, dry crumbs.

I closed my eyes. "We're here," I said to myself but also to Beryl. "We made it." I could see him beaming at me—his whole face shining just like that Statue of Liberty. A wave of longing washed over me. If only he were here, too, safe and starting a new life. In a strange way I felt as if I were saying good-bye to him all over again.

"We're here," I whispered, but this time it was to Pa. "Soon, Pa. Soon."

The sky grew slowly dark. When would they let us off the boat?

Suddenly without warning, BOOM! BOOM! BOOM!

Ear-splitting shots exploded around us. BOOM! BOOM! BOOM! They blasted from all directions.

I grabbed hold of Ma's arm. "What's happening? What is it?"

"Oh no!" Ma clutched us to her. "Oh no! What will we do? We're caught in another war!"

CHAPTER 26

BOOM! BOOM! BOOM! Blasts fired all around us. Flames exploded everywhere. I gripped Ma's arm. We huddled together as close as we could.

BOOM! BOOM! BOOM! Streaks of fire filled the sky. I pressed against Ma in terror. The air shook. I covered my ears but that didn't block out the terrifying blasts.

A man rushed over to us. "Don't be afraid," he shouted to us in Yiddish over the noise. "Don't worry!" Incredibly, he was smiling. With all this shooting, he didn't look frightened at all. "It's not a war," he tried to reassure us.

"No?" Ma kept her arms tightly around us. "Then what is it?"

"It's a holiday." He leaned in close so we could hear him over the noise. "People shoot off guns and fireworks and make all kinds of explosions. They call it the Fourth of July. Don't worry. No one's going to hurt you. They're celebrating their independence day."

So! That's what was going on—a holiday. What a day to arrive in America—July 4, 1921.

We watched in awe. Fireworks. What a lively place America was!

Now, more than ever, I wanted to live here. I wanted all these explosions to be *my* celebration, too, about *my* freedom.

Finally it was our turn to leave the boat. A man in a uniform asked Ma her name and checked some papers. Then he attached a little tag onto her dress. He did this for each of us. My tag he put on my shirt. I patted it. Everyone from steerage was getting one of these. So far, so good.

We walked down the gangplank—all six of us. I stepped proudly onto Ellis Island in my leather boots. I'd even shined them up with some spit. If only the shoemaker could see me now. My toes were pinched. But that didn't bother me. The Statue of Liberty had welcomed us. People had shot off fireworks when we arrived. Naturally, I wanted to look my best.

We found out soon enough that what Ma had heard was true. If we didn't pass something called a medical exam, they'd send us back to the *shtetl.*

"Let's not worry yet," said Ma. But those dark lines creased her forehead. I held her hand without any reminder.

We were taken to a big room where we waited in line with crowds of other people. Over against the wall, a whole family stood crying together—huddled around one little girl who was so pale and sickly, she looked gray. I recognized her from steerage. She was always throwing up. Ma said she must be too sick to stay in America. They'd marked a white *X* on the sleeve of her dress. She'd have to go back. But how could she? She'd barely made it here. How would she survive another trip? Would her whole family go with her? Or just her mother? Or, even worse, would she go alone . . . I prayed my hardest that such a thing wouldn't happen to any of us.

Finally, we were close enough to the front of the line to see a man in a white coat checking people over one by one. Someone said he was a doctor. This would be my first time ever being checked by a doctor.

Back in the *shtetl* there were no doctors. Ma had always made our remedies for us. If we had a bad cold, we wore a little cloth bag around our neck. Everyone did. It was filled with a thick, dark mixture of tar and cat droppings. It smelled something awful! But, with that nasty thing hanging on us, we got better as fast as we could. And until then, everyone stayed far away.

No one considered going to a doctor—not even the time Ma stepped on a piece of broken glass in the potato field and got a gash in her foot down to the bone. A neighbor lady wrapped a certain big leaf around Ma's foot and tied it on. She said it would make the foot heal. And after a few weeks, Ma's foot did get better. She'd never thought of going to a doctor. No one we knew ever did.

So here I was about to see my first one. And I wasn't even sick. The doctor motioned to me. I walked forward straight and tall and did my best to look as healthy as possible. But I was shaking inside. Ma stood right by me as he checked me over—inside my mouth, down my throat, in my ears. Now he was shining a light in my eyes. Next he was listening to my heart, and then my lungs. I was amazed. No one had ever paid this much attention to my body before.

Finally, he patted me on the head and smiled. He didn't send me over to the wall where the family was crying. He pointed straight ahead. A wave of relief rushed through me.

"A dank!" Thank you, I said in Yiddish even though, of course, he couldn't understand. But I gave him my biggest smile—which everyone understands.

I moved forward and before I knew what was happening, a lady in a white dress took my arm and stuck a needle into it. Ow! That hurt. Someone explained that it was supposed to keep me healthy.

How could a needle keep me healthy? It made no sense. But if that's what they believed here in America, I wasn't going to argue.

One by one, the doctor examined everyone in my family. And one by one, he nodded us forward to get stuck with a needle.

Every one except Benyomin. When the doctor checked

his eyes with that light, he kept looking and frowning, taking much longer than he had with the rest of us. Still frowning, he shook his head, took a piece of white chalk, and made an *X* on Benyomin's shirtsleeve. He motioned him to sit down and stay there.

Then he went over and spoke to one of the other doctors. I looked up at Ma. Her lips were pressed tight as she watched those doctors. The other one came over and looked at Benyomin's eyes, too. He frowned and spoke to the first one.

They talked for a long time. Benyomin sat there looking small and helpless, but not sickly like that little girl. Why were they keeping him? He wasn't sick!

I remembered one time back in the *shtetl* when he was truly sick and feverish. Someone had told Ma that the only way to get him better was to give him some mare's milk. So Ma had sent me to the market with an empty cup and a *groschen,* a small coin. I found a man with a mare and gave him the coin. He squirted some mare's milk into my cup. And I carefully carried it home, not spilling a drop. Benyomin drank it and sure enough, he got better. Of course, I never let him forget who got him that milk.

But here, it was completely different. Benyomin wasn't sick. Yet they'd put that mark on his sleeve. And there was nothing I could do to help him. Nothing any of us could do. The doctors kept pointing at his eyes and talking to each other in a language we didn't understand.

What were they saying? Benyomin could see just fine! If only we could tell them . . .

I looked over at the family huddled around the sickly little girl. How could they send anyone back? It was unthinkable!

The second doctor took another long, careful look at Benyomin's eyes. He talked to the first doctor. Finally, the first one patted Benyomin on the shoulder and smiled. He motioned him to go over and get stuck with a needle.

Benyomin jumped up and hurried so fast he almost tripped. He held out his arm and got poked before the doctors could change their minds. By the time he reached us, Ma looked as if she might collapse. But not me. I jumped up and down and gave Benyomin a punch on his other arm—right on that *X*.

"You almost got us sent back!" I scolded. "You should have told them you can see just fine. *I* would have!"

"Sure, sure," said Benyomin. "You and your big mouth."

Now we could joke.

"Come this way." A lady led us into a huge room with a big long table—the longest I'd ever seen in my life. "We have some food for you," she told us. And, to my amazement, it wasn't thin cabbage soup. No, this table was filled with food.

Food! Food! Food!

CHAPTER 27

I could hardly believe my eyes. There were stacks of white bread—rich people's bread—right in front of us and pitchers brimming with milk. There were some foods we'd never seen or heard of before, foods we didn't even know how to eat!

This was more food than we'd ever seen. And people, just like us, poor people, were eating it.

"Sit down," said the woman who'd brought us here. "Eat as much as you like."

Could this be true? Even the white bread?

No one had to invite us twice. We grabbed at the white bread as though it might disappear. We ate and ate, hardly even chewing. We stuffed as much into our mouths as we could and swallowed fast so we could stuff more in. We thought if we stopped for even a moment, they might think we were done and take it away.

But they didn't. They let us keep eating. This was our one big chance to eat. And we made the most of it.

We wanted to try everything. There was a dark, slippery purple food we'd never seen before. I watched how other people ate it. They spread it on bread with a knife. I spread some on my bread and took a bite. It was sweet and fruity. "Mmm. Try it." I handed it to Ma.

She took a bite. "It's delicious. Try some," she urged the others. We all loved it.

"It's jelly," someone told us.

"Jelly," I said with my mouth full of it. "Mmmmm."

"Try this," said Kvola. She'd spread some thick brown sticky stuff on another piece of white bread.

I took a bite. It wasn't sweet or fruity. It was thick and gooey and it stuck in my mouth. But I liked the taste. I drank some milk and ate more.

"It's called peanut butter," someone told us.

"Mmm," I said with a full mouth. "I like it."

We ate and ate.

"What's that?" I asked Ma and pointed to some clear, yellowish liquid in a pitcher.

"I don't know." She made a face. "It looks very strange to me."

Benyomin made a face, too. "You know what it looks like?"

He and I looked at each other and giggled. There was only one thing we knew of that was a clear, yellowish liquid.

"Don't drink it!" said Ma firmly.

But she didn't need to tell us. We knew better than that!

A lady pointed to it and said, "Apple juice." She motioned for us to drink. But we didn't dare.

We tried everything else though—especially the white bread. I ate until I was too stuffed to take another bite. But Benyomin kept eating. And when no one was looking, he stuffed bread into his shirtsleeves and down his pants legs.

"We'll eat for a month," he told Ma proudly.

"Be careful," she warned. "Or someone will catch you." None of us had forgotten about Kvola and that one piece of white bread. And here, Benyomin had taken so much that his arms and legs bulged out.

"Don't worry. I'll put it into our sack when no one is watching," he promised. Then he stuffed another piece of white bread into his mouth and swallowed fast, barely stopping to breathe.

Later that night, though, he wished he hadn't eaten so much. He didn't get beaten or even scolded. But he moaned all night long. "Owww! my belly. Uhh! my belly!"

Poor Benyomin. None of us knew that someone could get a stomach ache from eating too much. And from the sound of his groaning, I was glad I wasn't the one who'd discovered it.

By the next morning, though, he felt a lot better. And that was a good thing because we were brought back to that same long table. Again, we were allowed to eat as much as we wanted. We were about as close to heaven as anyone in this world can be. A tiny part of me even wished we could stay and eat like this forever. But a much bigger part was itching to see Pa. I took out his picture and traced my finger around his face. *Soon, Pa. Soon.*

That afternoon, one of the workers came over to Ma. "Mrs. Myzel, someone is here for you." My heart almost jumped out of my chest.

Ma's face lit up. "Hurry!" she called to us.

"Pa's here?" I asked, brimming with excitement.

"Hurry!" she said again, smoothing her hair. Then she smoothed mine and straightened my clothes as best she could. We rushed out to meet him.

There stood a man with short dark hair and no beard. He didn't look much like the photograph of Pa. Next to him stood a woman who wore a nice-looking dress but no kerchief, like Ma's, around her head. Ma ran over and gave them each a big hug. They spoke excitedly in Yiddish for a few minutes as the rest of us stood there wondering who they were. Finally Ma turned back to us.

"This is your Uncle Moishe," she told us. "He's your pa's brother."

"Welcome to America," said my uncle, beaming. "But I'm not Moishe anymore. Now everyone calls me Max."

Max. What a strange-sounding name. There was no such name in the *shtetl.* I wondered where he got it.

"And this is your Aunt Dvora," Ma went on. "Uncle Moishe's wife." I noticed that Ma didn't use Uncle Max's new name. But she swelled with pride as we each said hello.

Aunt Dvora burst out with a flood of questions. "How was the trip?" "Are you feeling all right?" "Did they give you enough food?" "Are you hungry?" She asked so many, so fast—too excited to wait for answers.

Even though they both spoke Yiddish, they didn't look like they were from the *shtetl*—Aunt Dvora with her stylish dress and Uncle Max with his short hair and clean-shaven face. They looked so different, so American. It was hard to imagine they'd *ever* lived in the *shtetl.* I wondered if Pa looked as American as this.

Then a sudden new and exciting thought came into my head. I wondered if *I* ever would.

Uncle Max led us outside. He strode over to an automobile and pulled open the door. "This is my car," he said. "You children sit in the back."

An automobile! We scrambled in—hardly believing it was true. No one in the *shtetl* drove an automobile, much less owned one. We had *seen* them in Warsaw. But I never imagined I'd *ride* in one. It seemed a lifetime ago that we'd been in Grandfather's horse-drawn wagon with him sitting up front, straight and tall. Everything about Grandfather, his long gray beard, his round black sheep's wool hat, and his *kaputah,* the long black coat he wore, had looked just right back there. But here, I realized, he would be completely out of place with everything so modern.

This was a whole new world. We drove along on smooth paved streets—no bumps, no ruts, no mud. We gaped at the big buildings and all the shiny black automobiles. I was jumpy to see Pa! Yet there was no mention of him.

Soon my uncle parked the car and announced, "Before anything else, you're all going straight to the bathhouse!"

"A bathhouse!" Ma clapped her hands over her heart and beamed. "Oh! A *mechaieh!*" My sisters looked just as pleased as Ma. But for me, washing wasn't all that exciting.

As we walked along the street to the bathhouse, we passed some children wearing clean, nice-looking clothes. They pointed at us and giggled among themselves. I looked down at my own clothes, which were ragged and dirty. Well, I couldn't do anything about them. *But,* I reminded myself, I *do* have fine leather boots—finer than any of *their* shoes. And I *will* get myself clean—just as clean as any of them.

At the bathhouse, I scrubbed myself until my skin was raw. I probably washed off a month's worth of dirt. Now those American children would have nothing to laugh at.

My uncle smiled and nodded as we came out. “Better. Much better!” But then he took another look at Benyomin and me and frowned. “No.” He shook his head. “Not so good. Look at your hair. You both need haircuts.” This was true. By now, our hair was long and scraggly. Ma hadn’t cut it in some time. “I’m not taking you home like this,” he announced. “You’re going to the barber.”

The barber? This was something new.

But soon, *snip, snip, snip,* I looked as American as any of those boys on the street. Now, at last, I was all set to see Pa.

CHAPTER 28

When we finally got to Uncle Max's house, it was filled with relatives. I never knew we had so many! They'd all come to meet us.

Aunt Dvora introduced us around. Aunts, uncles, cousins—my head was spinning. I looked at all the new faces trying to find the most important one. "Where's Pa?" I asked my aunt.

My cousins giggled. "Maybe he's hiding. Did you check under the beds?" They all burst out laughing.

"Don't tease," scolded my Aunt Dvora. She turned to me, "Don't you know that your pa lives in Minnesota? That's a long way from us, here in New York—a few days by train."

A few days? Another train? My heart sank.

"But don't worry. You're not leaving yet! We're keeping you here as long as we can." She winked at me. I tried not to show my disappointment. All this way and still no Pa.

Now Aunt Dvora insisted we tour the house. What a house! Separate rooms to cook and eat and sleep in, electric lights, faucets with running water and, best of all, a flush toilet and no long lines. When everyone else was busy visiting with one another, Benyomin and I sneaked into the bathroom and shut the door.

"My turn first." Benyomin grabbed the flusher and pulled down hard. It made a great *whooshing* sound. We stood at the bowl watching the water spin around and around, down the hole, and then back up again. Next was my turn. I pulled down hard. What an exciting sound. It sent shivers to my toes. We watched the water swirl. What fun! I hoped Pa had a flush toilet.

We kept taking turns until Aunt Dvora poked her head in. "So *that's* what you've been up to!" She shook her finger at us, but she was choking back a laugh. "Come see your ma and sisters."

She led us into one of the bedrooms, and my mouth dropped open. They were all in American clothes. Ma's cheeks glowed pink with pleasure. She and my sisters looked so fresh and pretty.

"Where did you get those clothes?" I glanced around hoping there might be some for me and Benyomin, too.

"Don't they look nice?" asked Aunt Dvora. "My girls and I found some dresses we don't need anymore. We thought your ma and sisters might get some wear out of them."

"You look so pretty," Benyomin told Ma.

"And so American," I added, looking around hopefully, again.

"Too bad there aren't any boy cousins your size," Aunt Dvora told us. So I tried not to think too much about clothes anymore.

But when the grown-ups were out of earshot, our cousins had plenty to say about it. "Your clothes don't fit right." "They're all raggedy." "You look like you're from the old country!"

Our American haircuts didn't seem to make as big a difference as I'd thought. I looked down at my clothes. Again, I noticed how worn and shabby they were.

"You look like foreigners—like you just came off the boat," they teased—as if that was something to be ashamed of.

Didn't they know that we *had* just come off the boat? What was the matter with that? Didn't they remember their own boat trip here?

Then I found out. No. None of them had come here by boat. They were all born here—*real* Americans—with clean, good-looking clothes that fit nicely. *But,* I noticed proudly, none of them had fine leather boots like mine. I stuck one out hoping they'd notice.

And sure enough, one of the girls saw right away. "Look!" She pointed. "Look at Fivel's silly boots!"

They clapped their hands over their mouths and burst into giggles. "No one wears boots like that except old men!" "Oh, how funny!" "Fivel looks like a little old man."

My cheeks burned. I tore out of the house, away from all their pointing and giggling. Stupid boots. I tried to kick them off but they were too tight. I sat on the ground and tugged. Stupid old-man boots. What would Pa think? Would he be ashamed of me? I tugged harder. Or, would he remember that in the *shtetl* these were fine, handsome boots? But what difference did that make anyway? I gave another tug. Nobody *here* knew or cared. I finally yanked them off and threw them way into the bushes. One thing I knew for sure. I'd never wear them again.

CHAPTER 29

I thought we'd leave for Pa's right away, but weeks went by and Aunt Dvora kept saying, "What! Leave? Not yet. You only just got here. Who knows when we'll ever see you again?" She'd take Ma's hands in hers. "It's so good to see you. Don't you want to stay a little longer?" How could Ma say no? So we stayed.

My cousins still teased me and Benyomin. "Why don't you wear some other clothes? If your pa sees you in those rags, he'll send you right back to the *shtetl.*" I hoped they were just teasing about that. But one day Uncle Max shook his head solemnly and told me and Benyomin, "I can't send you to your pa barefoot and looking like ragamuffins. No," he said firmly. "I won't do it." My stomach knotted. Then with a smile, he added, "Before you leave I'm buying you both some new clothes."

New clothes? We'd never had new clothes before.

That day he took us to a store and bought us each a whole new outfit including shoes. And no pinched toes either. We stared at ourselves in the mirror. American from head to toe.

Back at home, I showed off my outfit to my cousins. "See? Now I'm a real American."

"No you're not," they insisted. "You don't even speak English."

But *that* didn't bother me. Everyone here spoke Yiddish. And of course Pa would, too. I could hardly wait to see him. Uncle Max had finally gotten our train tickets. He gave them to Ma and then gave each of us a few shiny American coins for our pockets for good luck. At last, we were heading for the train station.

"Make yourselves comfortable," Uncle Max told us. "You'll see half the United States before you see your pa."

Well, at least we'd have good food this time. Aunt Dvora had packed us plenty. As we stepped onto the train, I held my breath—remembering our last train ride. But there were no rotten smells. And even better, there were lots of empty seats. I grabbed one by the window. Benyomin did, too.

"Look!" I turned to my sisters, excitedly. "We can all have windows, if we want." But when I did, people around me stared. Had I said something wrong?

"Maybe we shouldn't," Hannah said quietly, keeping her eyes down. She slid in next to me. But people stared at her, anyway.

"I think we can sit wherever we want," said Kvola firmly. She took a window seat. But people stared.

"Not so loud," Ma hushed us. And people stared at her, too.

Then I realized. It was our Yiddish.

Whenever I opened my mouth, I could feel their eyes and their thoughts. *Foreigners. Right off the boat. Outsiders.*

My cousins were right. Even with our new clothes and haircuts, anyone could tell we weren't American.

If only I could open my mouth and have English come out as if it belonged there. But I'd left that easy belonging far behind. I now had stiff new shoes and brand-new clothes and a whole new language to learn. How long would it take? Would my clothes and shoes still look new or would they be old and worn by then?

We sped by vast stretches of open fields and farms much bigger than any we'd seen on our ride to Vilna. I listened hard to the language that everyone else was speaking. It sounded new and promising like good food and plenty of it. It had its own rhythm like the hustle and bustle of American life—horns honking in polished black automobiles and guns going off for holidays instead of wars. Fresh, hopeful sounds, like the tap of brand-new shoes on paved streets and the clink of shiny, new coins in pockets.

I'd gladly trade all my Yiddish, Polish, and Russian—for this one language. If only I could!

Day after day we sped on.

"When will we get there?" I kept asking Ma—quietly so people wouldn't stare.

"We'll get there when we get there," she told me over and over. "Not until Duluth, Minnesota."

At each stop we'd wait and listen for the conductor to call out the name of the town. It was never Duluth.

Finally, at one stop, the conductor called out, "Minnesota." I looked out the window at the long stretches of green hills. Minnesota. This would be my new home. Then as if he'd heard my thoughts, the conductor announced, "Duluth."

"Get off!" Ma exclaimed. "Hurry—before the doors close. There's your pa!" Her voice trembled.

At that moment, I didn't care who heard our Yiddish or how much they stared. We rushed off that train faster than you could say, "Hang onto each other."

Ma hurried across the platform straight to Pa. She reached out to give him a hug as she'd given our other relatives but then stopped, as if suddenly shy. We all hung back, waiting.

"Aren't they happy to see each other?" I whispered, a little worried.

"Of course they're happy," said Kvola.

"But it's been such a long time," Hannah explained. "It will take a while for them to feel comfortable."

I don't know what Ma and Pa said to each other. They spoke too quietly for any of us to hear. But then Pa reached out and took Ma's hand tenderly in both of his. He drew it to his lips, his eyes never leaving hers. They were both in tears.

"That's my pa," I said to myself. "He looks like a very nice man."

Pa took out a handkerchief and blotted his eyes. "It's been a long time," he said and blew his nose hard.

"Too long!" I burst out.

"Fivel!" Pa exclaimed, as if he'd known me forever. He threw his arms wide open.

I ran into them. "Pa!" I held on tightly for a good long time.

"Just look at you!" He stepped back. "Nearly all grown up already!"

I stood as tall as I could to show him just how right he was.

CHAPTER 30

Pa brought us straight home to Sixth Street—to a real house, not a one-room shack. It even had a doorbell like Uncle Max's house.

As Pa led us proudly around, I kept gazing at his face, drinking it in. *Pa, my Pa.* He showed us from room to room, all the while holding Ma's hand in his. *What a nice man,* I thought.

The house had a kitchen with a faucet that brought in clean running water—not like the rusty outdoor pump in the *shtetl.* There were also two bedrooms and even a living room, all with electric lights. And just as I'd hoped, there was a bathroom with a flush toilet. The house was much smaller than Uncle Max's, but to us it was a palace. It gave me a wide, open feeling.

Pa smiled at our delight, still holding and patting Ma's hand. "We don't have much money. But we'll always have food."

"We've gotten by with far less," said Ma.

A look of sadness swept over Pa's face. "I know you have." He smoothed her hand. "We'll be all right. I have a job peddling rags. I don't earn much, but we won't starve."

"I'll find work, too," said Ma. "And the girls are old enough to get jobs."

"I will, too," I said—wishing Ma had thought of it.

"We'll see," she said. But Pa gave me a wink and a smile that lit me up inside. *My Pa.*

While Ma and Pa sat down to talk, Benyomin and I ran from room to room—trying to believe that this was really our home.

I looked out the window. Some children were playing hide-and-seek, a game we'd played in the *shtetl.* I tugged Benyomin over. "Let's go see if we can play."

"What if they don't speak Yiddish?" he asked.

"What if they do?" I countered. "Let's find out. Come on." I tugged his arm.

"No, you go if you want." He pulled his arm free. "I'm staying here."

I wasn't going to let Benyomin worry me. I ran outside. "Can I play?" I asked in Yiddish and motioned that I wanted to join in.

"Do you speak English?" one boy asked in Yiddish. He looked a few years older than me.

"Not yet," I said. "But I know how to play hide-and-seek."

They talked it over in English and finally the boy said to me, "All right. You can be 'it.' Come with us."

See? I thought to myself. Already *I* have friends. Too bad for Benyomin. They brought me a few streets down.

"Sit here." The boy pointed to the front steps of someone's house. "Cover your eyes and count. If anyone comes, just say, 'I did it.'"

So I practiced my first English sentence: "I did it. I did it."

"That's very good," he said. They all smiled.

I covered my eyes and counted.

The doorbell rang. I heard a scuffling of running feet, but I didn't peek. I'd show them that even if I didn't know English, I was still smart. I heard the door swing open.

I uncovered my eyes. All the children were gone. A lady was frowning down at me, hands on hips. One of her flower pots was on its side, with dirt and flowers spilling out. She pointed to it and said something in English.

"I did it," I said.

She gave me a very stern look. Right away I knew the children had tricked me. I didn't wait to find out what she'd do next. I flew down the steps. My heart raced me all the way home. The children were already there. "Ha! ha! You said, 'I did it.'" Oh, they thought it was so funny!

I laughed, too, hoping maybe they'd still want to be friends. But even while laughing, I thought to myself, they must think I'm dumb. Really dumb. I'm laughing just like Yusig—as if I don't know any better.

I remembered his quivery smile. And his sad, questioning eyes. A sudden thought came to me. It must've hurt *him,* too. But he'd laughed anyway. Now I knew how badly he'd wanted to fit in.

I'm sorry, Yusig—really sorry.

I'd never imagined America would be like this. Never.

CHAPTER 31

That Friday, our first *Shabbos* together, Pa invited all our Duluth relatives over for dinner. He brought home two big chickens. This was going to be an amazing feast.

Ma and my sisters looked so happy to be cooking with all this food. My mouth watered. I could hardly wait.

At the dinner table that night, I thought I'd burst with good feelings. There was so much of everything. Plenty of food, lots of relatives, everyone speaking Yiddish, and best of all, we were finally sharing *Shabbos* with Pa.

My ears perked up when I heard Uncle Ralph tell Ma and Pa, "School starts next week."

"There's a *heder*?" I asked, wondering if the teacher here had a big stick, too.

"It's not a *heder,*" he said. "And it's not just for Jews. It's for children of all religions—a public school for boys *and* girls. You'll learn to read and write English."

English? It was as if he'd reached right into my head and pulled out my biggest wish.

"But can we afford it?" Ma asked, worry already furrowing her brow. I glanced at our glass money jar on the counter. That's where Pa put his money from peddling rags. And we'd all put in our coins from Uncle Max. But there wasn't a lot. Ma was so careful with every coin she took out.

"Please, Ma," I urged. "If I learn English, I can get a job." I'd seen boys selling newspapers on street corners. With a little English, I could do that, too.

Pa smiled. He didn't seem worried at all. "The school is free." He beamed at all of us—as if he, himself, had made it so.

Free? For all children? It seemed unbelievable.

Pa looked pleased at our surprise. *What a nice man,* I thought again, as I had so often lately.

"So can we start next week?" I asked.

"Absolutely," said my pa. And there wasn't a single word spoken all evening that made me happier.

CHAPTER 32

On Monday, Uncle Ralph brought all five of us to Jefferson School. *I'm about to learn English,* I kept telling myself. *English.* I bounced up the steps two at a time.

In the school office, Uncle Ralph spoke in English to the woman behind the desk and then back to us in Yiddish. He makes it look so easy, I thought. Soon I'll be doing that, too!

"She wants to know your names," he told us. "But not your Yiddish names." He shook his head and made a face. "You all need American names." When he said *American* he puffed out his chest. We knew, of course, that Ralph was an American name. But we didn't know where he got that name or how we could get some for ourselves.

"Don't worry," he told us. "I'll figure it all out." He turned to Hannah and rested his thumb against his chin for a moment. "Your name will be Helen."

"Helen?" Hannah said it carefully. We'd never heard that name before.

"That's right." My uncle nodded. And the lady behind the desk wrote it down.

Then he turned to Kvola and said, "You'll be Eva."

To Rifka he gave the name Ruth. And Benyomin he said would be Ben.

Helen. Eva. Ruth. Ben. I'd have to practice to remember them. Of course, Ben was easy. But the others were so different from any names I'd ever heard before.

Finally my uncle turned to me. "Fivel, we'll call you Phil."

Phil. I liked it. There was no such name back in the *shtetl.* You could only get a name like that here.

"Phil," I said, enjoying the sound of it in my mouth. A clear, new sound. An American sound.

The lady behind the desk said something to my uncle.

He turned to us. "She needs to know how old you are so she can put you in the right class."

But none of us knew our ages. So my uncle and the lady decided where they thought we belonged. My sisters were all led down one hall. Benyomin and I were led down another.

"Here's your class," the lady said, opening the door for me. "It's fourth grade." And Uncle Ralph translated. I looked back at Benyomin, expecting him to follow. "He'll be in fifth grade," she told Uncle Ralph. "That's a different room."

"Wait for me after school," Benyomin whispered. I nodded and walked into my new classroom alone.

The children all looked about my size. So I figured I

was in the right place. They were all wearing nice fresh clothes. Thank goodness I was, too.

Luckily, there was one girl in the class who was Jewish and spoke Yiddish. Jeanette. The teacher sat me down next to her so she could tell me what was going on.

The first thing Jeanette told me was, "Miss Fiebiger just explained to our class that you don't speak English because you're a new . . ." she searched for the word in Yiddish, but finally said it in English, ". . . *immigrant.*"

"What's an immigrant?" I asked.

"It means you're from somewhere else—not America," she said. "You're the only immigrant in the whole school."

By now the entire class was staring at me. I wanted to hide under my desk. *Immigrant.* I didn't like that word. It didn't sound American at all.

"No," I told her. "I'm not the only one. My brother and my sisters are immigrants, too." That made me feel a little better. But I wished the teacher hadn't called me that.

Now she was handing out paper and telling the class something.

"Write down your birthday," Jeanette told me in Yiddish.

"My birthday?" But already, she was busy writing. All the children were, except for me. The teacher came over. She put her hand gently on my shoulder and spoke to Jeanette.

"Miss Fiebiger wants to know if you need help writing down your birthday," Jeanette explained.

"Yes." I nodded. "What's a birthday?"

As soon as Jeanette translated that back to the teacher, the whole class burst out laughing and talking at once.

I didn't need any translation to imagine what they were saying, "The new immigrant doesn't know what a birthday is!" "Oh! That's so funny!" "Ha, ha, ha." The tips of my ears went hot.

The teacher tapped her ruler and spoke sharply to the class.

Jeanette translated back for me. "Miss Fiebiger told everyone to stop laughing. She says there's a lot you still don't know because you're new here. But, by the end of the school year, you'll have learned so much that you'll be giving a speech just like the rest of us."

"A speech?" My mouth went dry. "In English?"

"Of course in English! It wouldn't be in Yiddish, silly." Jeanette giggled. But it wasn't the kind of giggle that made me feel stupid. It was more of a friendly giggle. Then she explained, "At the end of fourth grade, we each have to stand up in front of the class and give a ten-minute speech."

I couldn't imagine standing up in front of the class and saying even one English sentence—much less a ten-minute speech. But I was glad my teacher thought I'd be able to.

"It won't be too hard," Jeanette added. "It's always about family."

Family? What could I say about my family that wouldn't make me sound like an immigrant? Well, the end of the school year was a long ways away. Right now I had something more pressing on my mind. "What's a birthday?" I reminded Jeanette.

"It's the day you were born. You know, the day you celebrate each year. For homework, ask your mother when your birthday is."

Birthday. Another new word that I didn't like. I'd never celebrated anything called a birthday. There were no birthdays in the *shtetl*. But I was smart enough not to tell that to Jeanette. Now that I knew what it was, I'd just have to get one.

It wasn't long before the bell rang and everyone lined up. Miss Fiebiger led the class outside. I thought about my day. I'd learned two English words. And I hated both of them. *Immigrant.* No one else in my class was one. And *birthday.* Everyone else in my class had one.

I planned to quit acting like an immigrant as fast as I could. But I could see already that it would take some time. Birthdays were a different story. I could get a birthday right away. I headed for home in such a rush, I forgot all about Benyomin.

Jeanette came running after me. "Wait Phil," she called. "Where are you going?"

"Home," I shouted over my shoulder and kept running. "To get a birthday."

"No." She caught up, panting, and grabbed my arm. "Come back. You can't go home yet. School isn't over."

"It's not?" I stopped short. "Then why did the teacher let us out?"

"For recess."

"What's that?"

"It's when we play outside," she explained.

"You play outside at school?" This was hard to believe.

"Yes, come on. Hurry or we'll miss it."

We both raced back, and Jeanette explained to everyone, "He didn't know about recess."

Oh, they thought that was funny! They elbowed each other and laughed. Again, I could imagine what they were saying. "Phil, the immigrant, doesn't know about recess!" I tried to laugh, too. *Just like Yusig,* I thought.

Soon all the children were running around playing tag. This was a game I knew. So no one could tease me. I found Benyomin by the fence, watching.

"Come on, let's play." I grabbed his arm.

He held back. "We don't even speak English."

"That doesn't matter," I urged. "We can still play."

He wouldn't, though. He hung by the fence. But I wasn't about to. This was one thing at school that I could do! I joined in running around with all the others.

By the end of recess, I'd learned some more English and hadn't gotten caught once.

By the end of the day, I knew lots of words besides *immigrant* and *birthday.* I knew *paper, pencil, homework, recess, tag,* and *Wow! You're fast!* Not bad for my first day.

As soon as school really let out, I found Benyomin and we ran straight home. I couldn't wait to tell Ma my biggest news.

I burst into the house. "Ma!" I exclaimed. "I got a new name! It's Phil."

"Phil?" Ma made a face as if tasting rotten food. "I've never heard of it. What's the matter with Fivel?"

"It's not American," I told her. "From now on, my name is Phil."

"No." Ma shook her head. "Your name is Fivel."

This was not what I'd expected at all. So I tried to explain it to her. "Uncle Ralph says we need American names. He says my name is Phil."

"And he says mine is Ben," said Benyomin.

Then my sisters all arrived and told Ma *their* new names.

"That's enough!" Ma cut the air with her hands. "You all have good Jewish names that Pa and I gave you. I don't want to hear another word about these American names!"

"But we need American . . ." I stopped. Something about Ma's eyes—suddenly sad and lost—made me quiet.

"Well, anyway," I eased in carefully, "my teacher says I need a birthday."

"I do, too," said Benyomin.

"A birthday?" Ma looked annoyed. "What's that?"

"It's the day we were born," Benyomin told her. "We need to write it down."

"The day you were born?" Ma shook her head. "That was so far back. How can I remember?"

"My teacher says it's on my birth certificate. That's the piece of paper that tells the day I was born," Benyomin explained.

Ma wiped her hands on her apron. "There's no such paper." Her voice took on a sharp edge. "Back in the *shtetl,* we all knew we were born. We didn't need a piece of paper to tell us." She shook her head. "I don't understand all this about new names and birthdays. It's ridiculous."

"But we need a birthday for school," I reminded her.

Ma crossed her arms over her chest. "If you ask me, it's a little *meshuggeneh.* You were born, right? Isn't that good enough?"

"For the *shtetl,* it was good enough," I told Ma gently. "But here in America, it's different. Here, everybody has a birthday. If we want to go to school, we need one, too."

"Oh," said Ma quietly. "I see." She sat down at the kitchen table and thought hard. Finally, she turned to Benyomin. "I remember that when you were born all the church bells were ringing. There was only one day a year when they rang all the bells like that—Christmas."

Benyomin sure looked pleased. Now he had a birthday: December 25. Nice and easy. I hoped mine would be as simple as that.

Ma turned to me, "Fivel, I remember when you were born I ate *matzoh* ball soup. So you were born during *Pesach.*" Passover. She nodded with certainty. "That's the only time all year we ate anything made with *matzoh.*"

Well, this wasn't nearly as easy as Benyomin's birthday. Each year, Passover came at a different time. Sometimes in March, sometimes in April. When did it come the year I was born? Ma had no idea. We didn't even know what year I was born, much less the month or day. But, one thing I knew for sure. I needed a birthday by tomorrow. It was my homework.

The next day at school, I said to Miss Fiebiger, good and loud, so the whole class could hear, "My birthday is April 12." I'd practiced the English over and over with Jeanette.

"What year?" the teacher asked. "1912?" Jeanette translated back to me and then added, "That's when everyone else in our class was born."

"Yes," I said in English, "1912." And I thought to myself, good, now I have a birthday. And I'm already speaking in English. Boat or no boat, I'm becoming a real American.

CHAPTER
33

By spring, I'd learned plenty of English, including some bad words from boys on the playground. They'd taught them to me perfectly but didn't tell me what they meant. Instead, they'd say, "If you don't understand something, say this." And "If you need to go to the bathroom, say this."

Then when I used those words in class, Miss Fiebiger would raise her eyebrow. "Phil!" She'd frown. "Where did you learn *that?*" The boys would snort with giggles. And I'd know right away I'd been tricked again.

But by now, I could speak like any American boy—in class *and* on the playground. And I knew which words to use where. Just as I'd hoped, English now came out of my mouth as if it belonged there. More and more, I was becoming Phil, an American boy. Not Fivel from the *shtetl* anymore.

No more Hannah, Kvola, Rifka, or Benyomin either. Now it was Helen, Eva, Ruth, and Ben. And I made sure they called me Phil.

Eva and Ruth could chatter away in English. Ben and

Helen were both shy about talking and making mistakes. So it was taking them longer. But by now Ben knew more than enough English to join in the games on the playground.

Even so, I was the only one in my family who spoke without an accent, including Pa. Anyone hearing me thought I was born here. I was awfully proud of that.

Most of the time, Pa called me Phil—when he remembered. But Ma mainly spoke Yiddish and would only call me Fivel.

"I'm Phil," I'd remind her as often as I dared.

But she'd say, "To me, you're still Fivel and you always will be. So don't make a fuss about nothing."

She didn't understand that to me it wasn't nothing. Eva was the only one who really understood. She'd tried to get Ma to use her American name, too. "I just love the name Eva!" she'd say. "It's so pretty. Don't you think so, Ma?"

"Kvola is pretty, too," Ma would say.

One day, Helen drew us both aside. "It's not so easy for Ma, you know—a new language, new names, new everything." I figured Helen understood this better than any of us since, aside from Ma, she'd taken the longest to get used to being here.

Things did change for her, though, when Pa found her some paying seamstress jobs. Then she *had* to talk. By now, she was speaking more English every day and earning money for the family, too, which pleased her no end.

"I guess you're right, Helen," said Eva. "It's not easy for Ma. She can call me Kvola. I won't make a fuss anymore." And she gave up.

But I couldn't do that. I knew I should. But I wanted and *needed* to be Phil. Every time I heard that name, I felt more and more as though I belonged here. While with Fivel, I'd cringe inside and think, *immigrant, outsider, foreigner.*

One time, Ben said to me, "Remember Vilkomerski?"

"Sure I remember." I nodded.

"And look at us now," he went on. "We have it so good. Plenty of food." He patted his belly. "And even money."

It was true. There was always food. And by now, we both had jobs selling newspapers on the street corner before school. Every day we'd proudly drop our coins into Ma's glass money jar. We always tried to keep it at least half full and usually we managed to.

"Yes," I agreed with Ben. "We *are* doing well."

"So, don't make a fuss about a stupid name." Ben gave me a playful swat.

Part of me knew he was right and that part felt ashamed. But another part of me thought to myself, we're in America now. I want to be called Phil. Is that so terrible?

Sometimes Ruth called me Fivel just to tease me.

"Fivel! Oops!" She'd cover her mouth. "I forgot. Oh, I'm sorry, Fivel! Oh! Oops again!" She'd giggle, with mischief crinkling around her eyes.

She could tease any of us and get away with it. Even when she called me Fivel, she made me laugh. By now I couldn't imagine how we'd ever lived without her.

Recently, Miss Fiebiger had been explaining to the class about the ten-minute speech we'd all be giving soon. Even though I knew enough English, I was still nervous.

How could I talk about my family without sounding like an immigrant? Of course, I wouldn't mention anything about the *shtetl.* Still, I might slip and say *something* that, to me, was perfectly normal, but to the rest of the class sounded stupid.

Fortunately, I did have something exciting *and* American to talk about. Pa had just started working on a small farm in Matowah. He and the Finnish farmers out there all got along well. He'd even learned to speak some Finnish. He stayed there all week long and came home on *Shabbos* with lots of good stories to tell. My favorites were about the animals. The geese followed him around. The chickens pecked feed right out of his pocket. Even the bull calmed down for my pa. The farm would be perfect for my speech—as long as I didn't make any slip-ups.

There was only one boy in class who'd been excused from giving a speech. His name was Pekka. He'd just come from Finland this spring so he didn't know enough English yet. His ragged blond hair always fell in his eyes. And he wore the same clothes every day—as old and shabby as mine had been in the *shtetl.* I stayed as far away from him as possible.

The kids all poked fun at him. "Pekka, Pekka." They'd make squawking sounds. "Why don't you wear some other clothes?"

I knew it wasn't his fault about the clothes. But it did bother me that he didn't at least get an American name. That would be easy enough. Then he wouldn't seem like *such* an immigrant. But I figured it was his business if he wanted to keep such a strange name. At least now the class made fun of *him* instead of me.

One day, as the class went off to recess, Miss Fiebiger called me aside. "Phil, I have an idea for your ten-minute speech. You can talk about your family's life in Poland."

I wanted to say, *No! That's a terrible idea.*

But instead, I said, "I'm already planning to talk about my pa. He works on a farm now."

"The class knows about farms," said Miss Fiebiger. "But they don't know anything about your life in Poland. Please think about it." She said it nicely, but I knew I had no choice.

During recess, the boys were teaching Pekka one of those bad words they'd taught me months ago, explaining to him that he should say it to Miss Fiebiger if he needed help in class.

I was glad they had someone else to play tricks on nowadays. I might have even joined them, but I had more important things to think about.

CHAPTER 34

How could I give a speech about growing up in the *shtetl* and still sound like an American? I began to list in my head all the things I mustn't mention in my speech—hiding under the dirty old rug when Cossacks came, Ma stealing flour, us digging in the fields for leftover potatoes, Ben getting the fur hat off the dead Cossack. There were so many things. How could I avoid them all? And if I did, what was left to say? I'd just try to make it sound as ordinary as possible.

Finally the day of my speech came. I got up in front of the class, took a shaky breath, and tried to look calm.

"I was born in a little village," I began. "Smaller than Duluth. We lived in a small house. It was—well, sort of different from here." And immediately I wished I hadn't said that.

"What made it different?" someone asked.

"Well, there wasn't electricity," I explained. "And there wasn't as much food. One time, my sister Eva was working as a maid and she got beaten for taking a piece of white bread."

"She was a maid? Didn't she go to school?" a girl asked.

"Girls didn't go to school, and anyway we needed the money."

"How come girls didn't go to school?" another girl wanted to know.

"Because it was only for boys." The more I explained, the less they seemed to understand.

I still had time to fill, so I told about the Cossacks and how scary they were. "One time, my brother, Ben, almost got killed by a Cossack. But he was wearing a tall fur hat. And that saved him."

"If you were so poor, where did he get a fur hat?"

"Well, um, he . . ." I searched for how to say it. "He found it somewhere." But that didn't sound so good, so I tried again. "He didn't steal. He took it. It was um . . . on . . . um . . . a dead Cossack."

"There were dead Cossacks lying around and you just went and took their stuff?" I could tell he didn't believe me.

"What did *you* take?" another boy wanted to know. "A sword or pistol or something?"

I thought about that. Maybe I should tell them I took a sword *and* a pistol. They'd probably believe that more than the truth. But I wasn't sure Miss Fiebiger would. So I just said, "Some soldiers took the weapons. They just left the dead Cossack."

The boys in class looked disappointed but I went on, "That Cossack's hat saved my brother's life. You can even ask him."

"But why didn't the police arrest the Cossacks?"

"There were no police," I explained.

"No police?!" They couldn't imagine it.

"Then why didn't they get the sheriff?" asked another boy.

"What's a sheriff?" I asked. And immediately I knew I shouldn't have.

"What's a sheriff?" the boy snorted. And they all started laughing. "Phil doesn't know what a sheriff is!"

As always, I tried laughing, too. I was back to feeling like Yusig again and wishing my same old wish. If only I'd been born here. If only I knew the important things like sheriffs and not stupid things like Cossacks, which no one believed anyway. Then they'd have nothing to laugh at.

"Quiet!" said my teacher sternly. "Phil has been here less than a year. There's still a lot he doesn't know. But there's also a lot he does know." Her voice grew quiet and firm. "He knows what it's like to be hungry and afraid for his life."

I certainly didn't think that was anything worth knowing. But it did get the class to quit laughing. "We can all learn from each other," she went on. "Thank you, Phil, for telling us about your family's life in Poland."

On the playground that day, a group of boys from my class crowded around me. "What a story!" "You made it up, didn't you?" "How did you think of all that?"

"I don't know," I said, letting them believe what they wanted.

I wished I *had* made it up. I wished none of it were true or, at least, that I could forget everything—wipe it blank like Miss Fiebiger did with her blackboard at the end of the day.

I imagined a big eraser wiping away the whole *shtetl* from inside my head—making it all disappear. Blank. Then if any teacher ever asked me again, I could truthfully say, "I don't remember anything."

The only thing that made my day easier was when Pekka raised his hand and said his new bad word to Miss Fiebiger. I laughed louder than anyone. Miss Fiebiger gave me a stern look. But I kept laughing.

She raised her eyebrow at me. "Please stay after school, Phil."

CHAPTER 35

I hoped Miss Fiebiger wasn't angry with me. Maybe I'd been a little too loud. But was laughing such a terrible thing? She surprised me, though, with something totally different. "I'm sorry the class didn't believe you today, Phil."

"Oh, that's OK," I said, relieved.

"I guess it's hard for them to imagine such a different life," she went on.

"I guess so." I nodded. "Back in the *shtetl,* I never imagined a life like *this.*"

"Your life was very hard back there," she said softly. "I don't know how you survived."

"People helped us," I said, wishing I could just go home and be done with the *shtetl.*

But she nodded for me to go on and looked truly interested. So I told her about Ana and the old mittens and socks she used to give us and the small silver cross that saved our lives. Then I found myself telling all about Beryl and his bakery and how he'd kept us from starving.

"What extraordinary people!" she said.

"Yes," I agreed. "But the Cossacks killed Ana and her whole family."

"Oh . . ." Her fingers flew to her lips. "I'm terribly sorry."

"Beryl is still there, though," I added.

She gazed at me. "Just imagine if he could see you now. He'd be so proud of you." She patted my shoulder.

I nodded. But I thought to myself, I'm not so sure he'd be proud of me. I *do* know, though, that he wouldn't recognize me. Miss Fiebiger doesn't know how different I looked back then—shaggy hair, raggedy old clothes. And not only that, I *was* different. Since coming here, I really *had* changed. Everything had. But I couldn't possibly explain all that to her.

I walked home slowly, needing time to think.

Here, the children would laugh if I told them that our Sabbath soup from Beryl was our one good meal a week. They'd snort and say, "That wasn't a meal! That was just soup, silly!" But I knew the truth. It had saved our lives.

Everything about that life was so different from this one. I only knew one thing for sure: Fivel did not belong here.

Yet, as if disagreeing, my *heder* teacher's parting words came sharply back at me, *Fivel . . . don't ever forget who you are.* I could almost feel that stick of his threatening my head.

"I'm not Fivel anymore," I said out loud. "And I don't

want to be either." Again, I wiped the whole *shtetl* from my head with that big eraser. All blank.

"I'm home," I called as I walked through the front door.

"Fivel!" Ma greeted me from the kitchen. That name made a sour taste in my mouth—*immigrant, foreigner.* "You're home late," she went on in Yiddish. "Hurry and get ready for *Shabbos* dinner."

"I will. But please, Ma, call me Phil." I knew I shouldn't make a fuss about it—especially right before *Shabbos.* But somehow, I couldn't stop myself. "We're in America now. And that's my name."

Ma gave a not-this-again look and wiped her hands on her apron. "To me you're still Fivel."

Pa gave me a raised eyebrow so I let it be. He was home from the farm. It was always good to have him with us. I went over and gave him a big hug.

We all gathered around the dinner table. In my head, I called each of us by our American names: Helen, Eva, Ruth, Ben, and me, Phil.

We need these names, I reasoned with Ma in my head. We're not in the *shtetl* anymore.

I looked at the table all set for *Shabbos.* So different from back there. Plenty of food—a real feast. Then I caught myself. At school, the children would laugh at me for saying that. "Phil doesn't know what a feast is. Ha, ha, ha."

For them, this was just another meal.

How could the same food be two such different things?

For the first time in a long time, I thought back to how I used to gaze into the Sabbath candle flames and imagine Pa's face. He'd been so far away back then—impossibly far.

Now I leaned over and hugged him extra hard. "*Git Shabbos,* Pa."

He hugged me back. "*Git Shabbos,* Fivel, my boy."

"Phil," I reminded him.

Pa ruffled my hair. "Phil, Fivel." He shrugged. "What difference does it make?"

"A lot," I told him. "I want to be Phil, a real American. Not Fivel from the *shtetl.*" And I said Fivel and *shtetl* almost as if they were bad words.

A shadow of displeasure crossed Ma's face. But she calmly lit the candles and sang the *Shabbos* blessings.

I didn't want to think about the *shtetl.* It made me all mixed up inside. Until today, I hadn't even thought much about Beryl. And back there I'd promised to think of him every day. He had looked so pleased when I'd told him that.

But I'd been busy becoming American. I didn't have time. Now a terrible thought came to me. What if somehow, when I'd been erasing everything, I'd erased Beryl's face? That's all I had of him—a picture in my head. What if it was gone?

I gazed into the candle flames, closed my eyes, and got that same floating feeling I used to get with Pa. *Beryl, I want to see you.* But just as I feared, his face was gone.

Please, Beryl. I tried again. *Please.* But still nothing. I must've really erased him.

I squeezed my eyes tighter. *Beryl, I need to see you. I don't want to forget you.* And suddenly, there he was—just as always—with kindness filling his whole face. His smile seemed to say, Your new haircut and new clothes don't fool me one bit. You're still my Fivel.

My Fivel. That's just what he'd say, too. Not Phil. I suddenly realized, never Phil.

Quickly, before I lost the picture, I wrapped my arms around him. *Git Shabbos, Beryl.* And I thought to myself maybe right now he's thinking of me. I opened my eyes.

Ma gave me a rare, tender look almost as if she'd seen me hugging him right inside my head. "*Git Shabbos,* Fivel," she said. And strangely, it didn't bother me. In fact, though I can't explain why, being called Fivel suddenly seemed awfully important.

"*Git Shabbos,* Ma." I patted her hand, but it was more like *sorry* or maybe even *thank you.* I took a piece of *Shabbos* bread and ate slowly.

Now my *heder* teacher's words made real sense. *Don't ever forget who you are.* But who was I? Phil or Fivel? It was all too confusing. I only knew one thing for sure.

There was a great big ocean in between those two names. And no bridge.

But, as if disagreeing, the bridge to America popped into my head—just the way it used to back in the *shtetl.* I could see it as clearly as Beryl's face. My own bridge. And there I was walking on it. It made no sense, but somehow it did make sense. I could imagine myself walking back and forth across that bridge my whole life.

Maybe that's who I was. A boy with two worlds inside and a bridge that no one else could see.

The next day at school, boys on the playground were teasing Pekka again. "Pekka, Pekka." They made clucking sounds.

Later, when they'd finally left him alone, I went up to him.

"You need an American name," I told him, just as my Uncle Ralph had told me. "From now on, you'll be Peter." I grinned, hoping for a big smile back.

But he shook his head, ragged blond hair falling in his eyes. "No. I'm Pekka—like my pa and his pa. Not Peter. It's, it's not . . ." He struggled to explain. "It's not right." His face turned flat and lonely. "They're dead."

"Oh," I said, not knowing what else to say. Suddenly I really wanted to do something for him. "Well . . ." I tried again, "next time the boys teach you a bad word, I'll give you a wink—like this." I showed him. "Then you'll know not to use it in class."

Pekka pushed the hair out of his eyes and smiled. "Thanks."

"That's OK," I told him. I could almost feel Beryl beaming at me, even from a world away. "I know what it's like," I added. "I'm an immigrant, too."

AUTHOR'S NOTE

I was inspired to write *Bridge to America* after hearing Phil Myzel share rich and lively details of his remarkable life with my older daughter Laurel's sixth-grade Sunday School class in the fall of 1997. Although Phil is now a white-haired man, I could easily imagine him as a young boy. He still has a spring to his step, a mischievous sense of humor, and a vibrant, youthful spirit.

Now in his early nineties (he's really not sure how old he is and insists that he's still young), Phil continues to be active in the Duluth community. He's a retired newspaper photographer, reporter, and businessman. He worked his way from selling newspapers on the street corner to office boy and on up at the *Duluth News Tribune.* He's also a devoted family man with two daughters and three grandchildren. His beloved wife of 67 years, Pearl, passed away in 2002.

Phil regularly attends Torah study and services at Temple Israel and also sings in Temple Choir. For many years, he has blown the *shofar* (ceremonial ram's horn) for the High Holidays.

I interviewed him extensively as I worked on this book. Although this story has been fictionalized, all of it

This photo was taken in the shtetl, *with the family wearing borrowed clothes.* Top row, left to right: *Hannah, Fivel, Ma.* Bottom row, left to right: *Benyomin, Rifka, Kvola.*

is based on Phil Myzel's life. Most of the events did happen. Beryl, Ana, Tomas, Mira, Yusig, the shoemaker, and the *heder* teacher are all based on real people.

Occasionally, I had to "glue" some facts together with some fiction. And at times, I stretched or altered a fact for the sake of the story. For instance, there *was* actually a rich man who wanted to take Fivel. But he wasn't mean like the man in the story. He just wanted to help Ma because he saw how hard she was struggling. But Fivel's mother did firmly refuse to give him up. As in the story, Ma's daughter Rifka was living with Pa's parents. Fivel knew nothing about Rifka until they were reunited before their trip to America. It was after about seven years that Pa sent his family money, but it was not sent in a picture frame. The money was hidden in the bottom of a Quaker Oats cereal box. It was actually a neighbor lady who received her husband's photo in a wooden frame. She was so enraged that she threw it into the fire only to discover that there was money hidden underneath, bursting into flames.

Fivel (left) and Benyomin reunited with their father, Laib Isaac Myzel, in America.

Kvola *was* beaten for stealing a piece of white bread. And Beryl the baker did save many lives by adding extra food to many families' Sabbath soup pots. Fivel's neighbor Ana did give Fivel's family a small silver cross for their door—which saved their lives. Sadly Ana's entire family was killed. Benyomin's life was saved by a Cossack's hat. Fivel was actually almost thrown overboard halfway to the United States. And he did make up his own birthday once he arrived.

Phil in Duluth in his early twenties

Ma often told Fivel that he should grow up to be like Beryl with a big heart. Phil never saw Beryl again but he still remembers his kind face and gets tears in his eyes when he recounts the food Beryl put into all their soup pots. Phil himself has a big heart and does his best to include everyone.

When he was a young boy in the Duluth Public Schools, the other children did tease Phil and didn't believe his stories of life in the *shtetl.* There was no other immigrant, such as Pekka, in his class. Phil was the only one who got teased for being an immigrant. Back then, without much exposure to people from other countries

William Levine

Pearl and Phil Myzel on their fiftieth wedding anniversary

and cultures, his classmates found his stories too strange to be true.

Now, years later, I hope that readers will not only believe his story but will think of Fivel when they meet a new immigrant or when they hear about children in some part of the world who are struggling to survive in a war-torn country. Phil says that he was very much like any of the starving children in rags seen on the TV news. Each one has a story worth hearing that is different and remarkable in its own way.

HISTORICAL AFTERWORD

Poland, the country where Fivel spent his early life, has been occupied and controlled by surrounding countries at various times in its history. During Fivel's youth, Poland was controlled by three different countries at three different times. Fivel was born some time between 1911 and 1913. Russia controlled Poland until 1914 and had controlled it ever since 1795. Between 1914 and 1918, during World War I, the Germans occupied and controlled Poland. Fivel remembers that the Germans brought sacks of beans and other dried food to his *shtetl,* which helped keep the people from starving. He was probably about five years old at that time.

In 1918 the Germans were defeated and Poland gained independence. A Polish government was established. However, the government was very weak and Russia, which was in a civil war, hoped to regain power over it. At that time, Fivel was probably about six years old.

In 1920, when the story begins, the *shtetl* where Fivel lived was within Polish borders. The city of Vilna was the closest city to Fivel's *shtetl.* At that time, Vilna was part of Poland. However, it should be noted that Vilna (which is presently called Vilnius) is now part of Lithuania, which became an independent country in 1991. Vilnius is actually the capital of Lithuania.

When the story takes place, most Jews in Poland weren't fully accepted as Polish citizens. Legally Jews in Poland were citizens, but they suffered a lot of discrimination. "True" Polish citizens were Catholic and were native Polish speakers. Fivel's native language was Yiddish, the language of Jews in Eastern Europe. He also knew Polish (and some Russian). But since he was Jewish, not Catholic, he, like most Polish Jews, was treated as a second-class citizen.

At that time in history, Jews in some parts of Eastern Europe were told where they could and couldn't live. Most Jews lived in little *shtetls* and were very poor. (Fivel's family was particularly poor.) Although Jewish boys in the *shtetl* went to *heder* and studied the Torah (the Five Books of Moses) and learned to read and write Hebrew, most were not educated in other subjects. They were too poor to afford a higher education. Most Polish peasants were also very poor and were totally illiterate. At that time, Poland was a very poor country.

Meanwhile, in Russia in 1918, there was a civil war going on. The Red Russians (communist Russians) were fighting against the White Russians (those supporting the establishment). Both were trying to gain power over Russia and also over Poland.

Fivel's *shtetl* (which doesn't exist anymore) was located on a main road called Ragotke Road. The Red army and the White army were both trying to gain control of that road and also of the large bridge nearby, which would give them access to other parts of Poland. That's why so much fighting took place in and near Fivel's *shtetl*.

What about the Cossacks? The Cossacks were groups of Russian people who banded together and became fierce and brutal soldiers. Since they were so fierce, the White Russian army paid them to fight for them. During 1920 (when the story begins) many battles occurred near Fivel's *shtetl*. The Red Russians, the White Russians, the Poles, and the Lithuanians were all fighting for control of that area. Sometimes Cossacks fought for the White army. Sometimes the Cossacks changed loyalties (if they were paid to do so) and fought for the Red army. During that time, thousands of Jews were killed by the Cossacks and by the White army in terrible *pogroms* or massacres. Although most *pogroms* were in the Ukraine, there were some in Poland where Fivel lived.

It's no wonder that Jews were leaving for America—a place of religious and economic freedom—where people, no matter what their religious or economic background, could become citizens, work to improve their economic status, and enjoy all the rights and privileges of citizenship. The United States was, and still is, considered the land of opportunity for people from all over the world who want to share the freedoms that United States citizens enjoy.

ACKNOWLEDGMENTS

I wish I could acknowledge all the people who have helped me with this book. However, there have been so many children and adults who have shown an interest, encouraged me, and cheered me on during the seven years that I've worked on it that I couldn't possibly name them all, although I am grateful to all of them. There are some, however, I must name.

First, and foremost, I want to thank Phil Myzel for sharing his life stories with me and good-naturedly allowing me to fictionalize them. He continues to inspire me with his big heart, his love of people, and his positive spirit. He's encouraged me and believed in me from the very start and has been full of enthusiasm for this project all along the way. I also want to thank Phil's family for their appreciation of my efforts to capture the spirit of Phil's early life story.

Many thanks to my wonderful community of friends (adults and children) at Temple Israel in Duluth, for the countless ways they've given me support.

Thanks to my friend Jeanne Miller who, as my first reader, lavished me with her enthusiasm and her belief in the value of this story—which sustained me through more drafts than I can count.

My thanks to writing group members Katharine Johnson, Margi Preus, Rae Tyllia, Ann Treacy, and Maryann Weidt for all their help and insights, and for playing such an essential role in my writing life.

Thanks to Kathy Tucker, who saw the value of this story in its beginning stages and encouraged me to keep working on it.

I wish to thank the Arrowhead Regional Arts Council for awarding me a McKnight Artist Fellowship to work on this project. The funding and the award itself supported me during a time when I really needed it.

Thanks to June Perry for graciously setting the stage for me to read my early draft to her class at Lester Park School. And thanks to that class, Mrs. Perry's fourth graders of 1998, my first audience of kids, for their input and excitement, which helped me slog through many more drafts. My thanks to Duluth Public School ISD 709 for their Endowment Grant, which funded my visits to June Perry's fourth-grade class the following year—1999. And thanks to that class for its input and encouragement as well.

I'm grateful to Mary Casanova for her astute and generous guidance on the manuscript. It was a real gift to have my work taken seriously by such an accomplished writer. And I'm grateful to my cousin David Karol for his thoroughness in explaining the history of the times and for patiently and unsparingly assisting me with the Historical Afterword.

Thanks to Joanne Sher for sharing her genealogical expertise with me. Thanks also to Gail Cohen for her careful and invaluable copy editing. And thanks to my friend Andy Therien for jumping in to help when computer problems threatened to overwhelm me.

My gratitude to Dr. Ofer Nur, a historian at the Center for

Jewish Studies at the Ecole des Hautes Etudes en Sciences Sociales in Paris, for checking the entire manuscript for accuracy, for sharing his historical and cultural expertise, and for answering my many questions. (Any errors in the book are mine alone.)

A big thank-you to my editor, Ann Rider, for sharing my vision for this story and for her kind, insightful, and generously appreciative style as we worked on this book together.

Many, many thanks to my mother, Eleanor Glaser, and my sister, Barbara Glaser, for being there in the countless ways that they are. I want to acknowledge my father, Jerry Glaser, who always encouraged me to do what I truly cared about. I also want to acknowledge my four Jewish grandparents who, like Fivel's family, came to America from Eastern Europe, leaving behind everything familiar in order to create a better life for themselves and for those who came after them. Although this is not their story, their life as Jewish immigrants informed my childhood, richly flavoring it with Yiddish and with Jewish traditions. That flavor can be found in every page of this story. They are Isadore and Lillian Koral, Max and Dora Glaser.

And to my husband, John Herold, and my daughters, Laurel and Charlotte, who have seen me through more rejections and rewrites than any of us cares to remember, thank you beyond words.

GLOSSARY OF YIDDISH WORDS AND PHRASES

Yiddish is a language that has been spoken by Jews in some parts of Europe since about the tenth century. It further developed as a language when Jews settled in Eastern Europe during the fifteenth century. It is still spoken today by some Jews of that descent but mainly by older Jews and Jews in ultra-Orthodox Jewish communities. It is a colorful language with a lot of flavor and nuance, mainly made up of Medieval German, Hebrew, and Polish. For more about Yiddish, treat yourself to *The Joys of Yiddish* and *Hooray for Yiddish* by Leo Rosten.

In the *shtetl,* Yiddish was the language that Jews spoke to each other. It was the first language that Jewish children learned. However, it wasn't their only language. Fivel and his family also spoke Polish, the language of Poland. Plus they knew some German, which is similar to Yiddish. And they knew some Russian.

Yiddish is written from right to left and uses letters from the Hebrew alphabet. Thus, there is not one correct way to spell Yiddish words using our alphabet. The Yiddish words in this book have been "transliterated"—written the way they sound. However, in Yiddish, **ch** is pronounced with a guttural sound. It sounds like softly clearing the throat or gargling. That is how to pronounce the **ch** in *me**ch**aieh, Pesa**ch**, Shalom alei**ch**em,* and *A**ch**!* (which is actually German in origin). The same **ch** sound is made when pronouncing the **h** in ***h**eder.* The names in this book that are Yiddish—such as Beryl and Vilkomerski—are also spelled as they sound.

A dank: thank you

Ah lebmeh dine kuppaleh: literally means "a life on your head." But it's usually translated as "a blessing on your head."

Ai, yai, yai: an exclamation that can express many feelings including happiness and sadness.

Bagel: a hard roll with a hole in the center. Although bagels are common nowadays among people of all ethnic backgrounds, they were originally a Jewish food.

Feh!: an expression of disgust or distaste

Git Shabbos: Good Sabbath. This is a Sabbath greeting.

Git tog: Good day. This is a greeting.

Groschen: a coin of small value, such as a penny.

Heder: the traditional school where Jewish boys learned to read and write Hebrew and to chant the Torah—the Five Books of Moses. Traditionally Jews believed that the

Jewish community should provide an education to every Jewish boy—even the poorest. This is why Fivel and Benyomin were able to attend *heder.*

Kaputah: a long black coat worn by Jewish men in the *shtetl.* It is still worn by some very Orthodox Jewish men today.

Kiddush cup: a ceremonial silver cup used when blessing the wine during the Sabbath and other holidays.

Klop: hit

Klug: smart

Matzoh: unleavened bread, which tastes like a dry, bland cracker. Traditionally Jews don't eat leavened bread or anything that contains leavening during the Jewish holiday of Passover. Instead, Jews eat *matzoh* during the eight days of Passover.

Mazik: a mischief maker, an imp—usually used in an affectionate way.

Mechaieh: great pleasure, real joy, blissful enjoyment. It literally means "putting life into."

Mensch: an exceptionally fine person. Calling someone a *mensch* shows great respect for the person's character. It is the highest compliment you can give someone. It has nothing to do with the person's wealth or education. Rather it means that this is a high-quality human being—someone who is generous, helpful, responsible—

someone who does good deeds for others and who helps the community in times of need.

Meshuggeneh: crazy

Nu: So? Well?

Oy: an exclamation that can be used to express, with *feeling,* a wide variety of emotions.

Pesach: Passover. This is a Jewish holiday that comes in the spring. The holiday commemorates the biblical story of when the Jewish slaves fled Egypt. They left quickly and had no time to let their dough rise. Their bread remained unleavened—this is *matzoh.* Now, during Passover, Jews eat *matzoh* to commemorate the time of Exodus and to think about the meaning of freedom. Passover sometimes falls in March, sometimes in April. This is because Jewish holidays don't have a set date on the solar calendar (the calendar used worldwide nowadays). Instead, Jewish holidays are based on a lunar calendar. The changing dates of Jewish holidays explain why Fivel didn't know when his birthday was, even though Ma remembered that he was born during Passover.

Pivne: a bar or saloon

Pogrom: a massacre of Jews; the ransacking of Jewish villages and homes and the killing of Jews in Eastern Europe, since the Middle Ages through World War II but especially during the Crusades. They also occurred in the seventeenth century, and the late nineteenth and early twentieth centuries.

Shabbos: the Jewish day of rest. *Shabbos* starts on Friday just before sunset when the woman of the house lights the candles and sings the Sabbath blessings. Traditionally, no work is done—not even lighting a fire or cooking. It's a holy day set aside each week for peaceful rest, prayer, and study. *Shabbos* ends on Saturday at sundown.

Shalom aleichem: a traditional greeting such as "hello" or "how do you do" that literally means "peace to you." The customary response is to reverse the words, *Aleichem shalom* ("And to you, peace"). Traditionally, they are said when meeting and also when parting.

Shofar: a ram's horn that is blown in the synagogue on the High Holidays of Rosh Hashanah and Yom Kippur. The ceremonial blasts of the *shofar* are of different lengths and sounds—some high, some low. It's a challenging instrument to blow.

Shtetl: a small village in Eastern Europe that had either all Jews or mostly Jews. There were many *shtetl*s (the plural in Yiddish is actually *shtetlach*) all over Eastern Europe until World War II. None of them exist anymore, including *Vilkomerski* where Fivel lived. The Jews in the *shtetl* were generally poor and had a hard life as did the peasants who lived in the surrounding countryside. Fivel's family was exceptionally poor. Life in the *shtetl* was very isolated from the outside world. It didn't "keep up with the times." When the story takes place, the *shtetl* where Fivel lived was located within the borders of Poland as was Vilna—the closest city. However, in present day, Vilna is the capital of Lithuania.

Shtickel: a little piece of something

Tsu reiss gezunterate: "Tear them in good health" is an expression used for new shoes. It's another way of saying "wear them in good health." It means "stay healthy so you can run around and wear out your shoes."

Tsuris: troubles, worries, or problems

Zayde: grandfather

Zisseh: sweet

Zisseh tsuris: sweet problems or sweet troubles—problems that come from happy situations, such as having so many good books to read that there's not enough time. Everyone should have such *zisseh tsuris*!